The trail of flights and accommodations that had been constructed for the fictional Dana Wright's travels was convincing, but if the time ever came that Norbert Cummins saw me face to face he'd know at once that I wasn't his younger sister.

I wondered, if I were Norbert, what I'd do in that situation.

Say, "You're not my sister. Oh, well . . ." and walk off.

Or kill me anyway?

Given that he had nothing to lose, and was a certified lunatic anyway, I guessed he'd kill me, right there and then.

Unless I got him first.

LOOKING FOR NAIAD?

Out of Sight

A Denise Cleever THRILLER

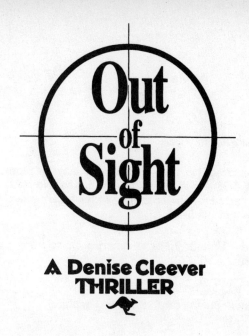

Out of Sight

A Denise Cleever THRILLER

Claire McNab

THE NAIAD PRESS, INC.
2001

Printed in the United States of America on acid-free paper
First Edition

Editor: Lila Empson
Cover designer: Bonnie Liss (Phoenix Graphics)

Library of Congress Cataloging-in-Publication Data

McNab, Claire.
  Out of Sight : a Denise Cleever thriller / by Claire McNab.
    p.   cm.
  ISBN 1-56280-268-2   (alk. paper)
  1. Women intelligence officers—Fiction.   2. Australia—Fiction
3. Lesbians—Fiction.   I. Title.
813'.54—dc21

For Sheila

Acknowledgments

Three wonderful women, Lila Empson (editor), Judy Eda (proofreader), and Ms. X (typesetter) have done it again. Thank you!

ABOUT THE AUTHOR

CLAIRE McNAB is the author of thirteen Detective
Inspector Carol Ashton mysteries: *Lessons in Murder,
Fatal Reunion, Death Down Under, Cop Out, Dead
Certain, Body Guard, Double Bluff, Inner Circle, Chain
Letter, Past Due, Set Up, Under Suspicion,* and *Death
Club.* She has written two romances, *Under the
Southern Cross* and *Silent Heart,* and has co-authored
a self-help book, *The Loving Lesbian,* with Sharon
Gedan. She is the author of three Denise Cleever
thrillers, *Murder Undercover, Death Understood,* and
Out of Sight.

In her native Australia Claire is known for her
crime fiction, plays, children's novels, and self-help
books.

Now permanently residing in Los Angeles, she
teaches fiction writing in the UCLA Extension Writers'
Program. She makes it a point to return to Australia
once a year to refresh her Aussie accent.

CHAPTER ONE

On Wednesday I left Australia as Denise Cleever, anonymous public servant. I returned on Friday as Dana Wright, only surviving daughter of the notorious Edmund and Salvia Cummins-Wright.

Even though it was just after six in the morning, several international flights had already landed at Sydney airport, and drooping travelers in long queues were clutching various items of cabin luggage, duty-free purchases, passports, and customs declarations.

When I finally made it to the head of my line I smiled at the official standing behind the high counter and wished him a moderately buoyant good morning. His glance slid over me with practiced, weary boredom, but when he flipped open the passport I handed him, his expression changed to narrow-eyed concentration. Surely it couldn't be the photograph, which deliberately depicted me with blank-faced torpor. And certainly the passport itself was genuine, having been issued by the Australian government. Perhaps he recognized my assumed name, although the Cummins-Wright family was far more infamous in Britain than here.

He tapped my photograph with a blunt forefinger, the nail of which I noticed had a crescent of grime. "You Dana Wright?"

"That's what it says."

My airy tone didn't go down well. His frown deepened, although that may have been because someone in my queue, clearly an Aussie, yelled, "Get a move on, mate! We haven't got all bloody day."

"Step to the side," my official said.

"Is something wrong?"

He jerked his head. "Over there."

Another man, red-faced and officious, appeared. They conferred at length. An impatient muttering behind me made it clear my fellow travelers weren't happy. The next in line, a globular woman with a baseball cap and a T-shirt that read, WARNING: I HAVE AN ATTITUDE AND I KNOW HOW TO USE IT, lived up to these words by snarling in a nasal New York accent, "Shit! How long are these assholes going to keep us standing here?" She glared at me. "If you can't get your documents straight, then you shouldn't be flying." Her mouth turning down in righteous condemnation, she added, "Or drugs. Is it drugs?"

2

I gave her a confiding smile. "Heavens," I said, "it's hard to say. Could be either."

"This way, please," said the second official, indicating that I should accompany him. He had my passport and entry documents safe in one beefy hand. "You can bring your things with you."

Obedient, I followed him, aware that a third uniformed figure, a woman, had fallen in behind. This was all seriously irritating. The whole idea had been for Dana Wright to enter Australia like any ordinary Aussie who'd been abroad. True, apart from two visits to see friends, Dana hadn't returned to her own country for ten years, but I had a good ear for accents, and a voice coach in Los Angeles had given me a quick couple of lessons, so I was pretty well secure that I'd got the slightly clipped intonation that living for some time in Britain would produce.

The very last thing I wanted to reveal was that I was working undercover for ASIO — the Australian Security Intelligence Organization — but if the alternative was a strip search, I was going to be very tempted.

The three of us, me sandwiched in the middle, walked down a corridor of identical closed doors, our footsteps clicking a staccato beat on the polished gray surface. "Exactly what is this all about?" I asked, using a tone of polite outrage.

The stocky guy at the front halted at an anonymous white door. "In here," he said, handing me my passport and documents. Faintly smiling, he turned the handle and waved me inside. "Have a good day, Ms. Wright."

The door snapped shut behind me. There was only one person in the stark little room: my ASIO control,

Livia. It wasn't her true name, because it changed with every new mission. With a little ferreting, I'd discovered she was really Cynthia, although to my mind she deserved something rather more edgy and interesting — Justine, perhaps, or maybe Zaneta.

I put down my hand luggage — an overnight bag and an expensive, brand-name shoulder bag. Dana might support antiestablishment groups, but her clothes and possessions were top of the line.

There was a pause while we regarded each other, me standing, Livia seated at a rectangular table, her thin arms folded to rest on its bare polished surface. As usual, she looked totally at ease, as though it could only be perfectly normal to have me yanked out of an immigration line and marched off to see my control.

I didn't speak, and my expression didn't change. It was part of my training never to react if there were an unexpected meeting with a fellow operative, control, or instructor outside ASIO walls. I glanced around the windowless white room, then back at Livia.

"Sit down, Dana," she said, her expressive face split with a grin. "The room's clear. We can speak freely."

Livia had been calling me Dana from the moment that I'd been assigned to the mission six weeks ago, a short time after the real Dana Wright had lapsed into a coma after a climbing accident in Scotland had sent her plunging down a cliff. Now *I* was Dana Wright, activist and suspected terrorist, twenty-four hours a day.

I pulled out a chair, saying, "I was preparing myself for the indignity of a strip search." The thought

4

crossed my mind that if Livia happened to be the person in charge of such an activity, perhaps the experience might be . . . interesting.

She was an enigma to me, and I've always been challenged by mysteries. Spiky-haired, angular, yet graceful. She was older, I thought, than she looked. Of course fraternizing with one's control was strictly forbidden, but I'd bent the rules before —

"Something's come up."

"Bad?" It would have to be serious for Livia to be here at all. "We're not going to abort?"

"Norbert Cummins has escaped."

I stared at her. "Dana's brother. But isn't he —"

"In an asylum for the criminally insane?" Livia spread her hands. "He *was*. But not, it seems, any more."

This wasn't quite as catastrophic as I'd feared. Norbert had been incarcerated in Britain after a trial for killing his parents and one of his sisters. Found not guilty by reason of insanity, he was put away at Her Majesty's pleasure, which, in effect, meant life imprisonment for Norbert. Now he'd be on the run, his face in every news report, so the chances of his making it to Australia seemed remote.

"How did he get out?"

"Like any intelligent psychopath, he presented himself as well on the way to recovery. Sweet-talked a new, young psychiatrist into believing that he no longer posed a threat, and at the first opportunity bashed the guy so violently he left him with permanent brain damage, changed into his clothes, and walked out of the place as the doctor. Smooth as silk.

He'd been there long enough to know the routines, the security checks. Got away clear in the doctor's Jag."

Livia's face was somber. I quailed at the thought of giving up the mission when I'd spent so much time and effort becoming Dana Wright. "Hey," I said, "Norbert's half a world away. He isn't going to make it to Australia. I reckon he'll be arrested any time."

When Livia didn't look convinced, I added, "And I'll be safe in the middle of nowhere. Besides, why do you think he's looking for his sister, anyway?"

Livia tilted her head, pursed her lips. "As part of his treatment, Norbert Cummins kept a diary. The final entry says: 'Three down and one to go. There's only Dana left.'"

CHAPTER TWO

"Why would Norbert want to hurt his sister?" I asked. "She paid a fortune for his defense."

"Not hurt — *kill* his sister. And he doesn't need a logical reason. You might as well ask why he butchered the rest of the family."

I didn't have an answer for that, so I said, "Well, I'm in no danger. Norbert has everything stacked against him. His face will be in every British newspaper, so he'll go to ground. He doesn't have the contacts to find out where his sister has supposedly gone, and even if he did, he's got a snowball's chance in hell of getting out of Britain."

"Norbert Cummins is a sociopath," said Livia, as though that explained everything.

It's times like this I'd like to be able to raise one eyebrow in a cool, sardonic manner. As so far I've not been able to master this skill, I shrugged elaborately. "So?"

"He'll use anything, and anybody, to get what he wants. He doesn't feel anxiety or fear the way you or I would, but he can mimic very well the behavior of a normal person. You've seen the family history — he has had a long career of manipulating people to get what he wants. He can seem to be the most charming, caring man you've ever met."

Livia was taking this rather too seriously, I decided. I said lightly, "So he's a classic psycho. You're not telling me anything I don't already know."

She gave an impatient sigh. "You know what he's capable of — you've seen the crime-scene photographs, Denise."

"It's Dana," I said. The slip she'd just made with my name persuaded me she was truly worried. Livia didn't make mistakes like that. "I'll be super careful. One hint that he's anywhere around, and I'm gone. Okay?"

"Really? In the wilds of the Kimberleys?" Livia said scathingly. "Just like that you're going to trek out by yourself, are you?"

Her caustic tone was well-deserved. The Kimberleys, situated in the far northwest area of

Australia, contained country so rugged and remote that it could swallow up a thousand people and not burp.

"Look," I said reasonably, "Not only will Norbert not make it to the Kimberleys, but if he did, he wouldn't be able to locate me. Hell, ASIO doesn't even know for sure where the terrorist training camp is, so how could Norbert Cummins?"

Livia drummed her fingers on the table. Her fingers stilled, and she gave me a sharp nod. "All right, we'll go ahead as planned." She reached down to a briefcase and came up with a folder. "Here are some recent shots of him. He'll almost certainly change his appearance, but this is what he looked like when he escaped."

Norbert Cummins was handsome — no, he was beautiful, in a totally masculine, jut-jawed, blue-eyed sort of way. In two of the photos Livia handed me he was smiling, his expression little-boy mischievous, his eyes crinkled fetchingly, his teeth regular and white.

There'd been several photographs of him in the Cummins-Wright file I'd studied, and even the mug shots when Norbert was arrested for murder showed his astonishing good looks, although his expression had been blank — at that time for once he hadn't been trying to charm anyone.

Knowing that there was a remote possibility I might run into the man, I looked carefully at his ears, which were small, set close to his head, and had almost nonexistent lobes. A person accomplished at disguise could change the appearance of many features, but ears were usually disregarded. I mean, who looks at ears? And besides, they were very difficult to change convincingly — except maybe for Mr. Spock.

I pushed the photographs back across the table. "Okay."

"Do you need to look at anything in the file again?"

I shook my head. "Know it by heart, practically."

I wasn't kidding. To be convincing in my role as Dana Wright I had to know the history of the Cummins-Wrights as if I were a member of the family. There must be no chance that I could be caught out by any detail about her parents, her siblings, or her own life.

It would be maddening if I never needed to use all this information, although the family story was interesting in its own right. When, thirty-five years ago, Edmund Wright had married Salvia Cummins, it had been a conventional step for two proudly nonconformist people. Edmund had been born in England, the only offspring of a Tory politician and a distant relative of the royal family.

By the time Edmund Wright hit his twenties, his left-wing proclivities had become such an embarrassment to his father that he was shipped off to Australia, where he could do less damage. In Sydney he established a high public profile as the owner and editor of *Duplicity*, a radical publication whose masthead proclaimed: WE REVEAL THE LIES THEY TELL YOU: THE TRUTHS THEY HIDE FROM YOU.

Salvia Cummins was an American, a black sheep in a family of white ones, all of whom were dedicated to making the family manufacturing business successful. After a tumultuous time at university, Salvia eventually joined an international protest group, traveling from country to country demonstrating against multinationals and their influence over local politics.

Edmund and Salvia met in Sydney, and it was a match made in heaven — had they been willing to acknowledge that such a place might exist. Their children were to bear the Cummins surname if male, and the Wright name if female. In due course Salvia produced four children: Elliott Cummins, who died in infancy; Philippa Wright; Norbert Cummins; Dana Wright.

When Dana was in her mid twenties, Edmund's father, now a widower, died, leaving his only son a considerable inheritance. The family returned to England to move into Wright House, a large — and from photographs, an excessively ugly — country house in Sussex.

True always to their beliefs, Edmund and Salvia poured money into causes dear to their hearts, financing radical groups, providing accommodation for visiting zealots, paying the legal costs of individuals arrested for extremist acts, as well as being deeply involved in protests and demonstrations themselves. Phillipa and Dana Wright followed their parents' lead, becoming, if possible, even more rabid in their ideology. Phillipa trained as a lawyer, specializing in political causes; Dana completed a degree in communications. Phillipa dated; Dana remained exclusively wedded to the cause.

It would have been a happy anarchist family, but for Norbert Cummins. He clearly had no intention of working for a living, and, using the accomplished charm that worked so well for him, he continued the wastrel ways he had honed to a fine art growing up in

Sydney. Entirely without conscience or any ethical standards, Norbert lied, cheated, and generally deceived everyone with whom he came in contact. His specialties were enchanting middle-aged ladies so he could swindle them, and seducing young women unfortunate enough to fall under his spell. He also showed a tendency toward extreme violence, and only the intervention of his parents, plus the application of considerable funds to injured parties, saved Norbert from serious legal charges.

The events that would lead to the deaths of Edmund, Salvia, and Philippa began with a series of bitter arguments with his parents. Disgusted that Norbert not only refused to subscribe to the correct radical doctrines, but that he also had lately begun to publicly mock Edmund and Salvia's activities, his parents took him to task. Norbert refused to see reason, and his tirades against his parents intensified to the point where Edmund was driven to cancel his son's considerable allowance and turn him out of the house.

At the trial, the housekeeper had given a chilling account of Norbert's reactions: "He just stood there, looking at his parents, cold like, not saying a word. Then he sort of smiled and nodded slowly at them, and said, ever so softly, 'I'll come back and get all of you. Believe it.'"

Two days later on a mild summer night, Norbert broke into the house, hatchet in hand. In a bloodbath that crime-scene photographs showed in sickening detail, he dispatched his mother, father, and sister Philippa with hideous savagery. Ironically, the CIA saved Dana, who escaped being hacked to death because she'd gone to London to join an all-night picket at the Savoy Hotel, where the head of the CIA happened to be staying while attending meetings on international security.

From the media's point of view, Norbert Cummins' trial was the ultimate news event, containing such winning elements as a handsome, charming accused — he had his own cheer squad of dimwitted women who attended the proceedings every day — plus victims who were notorious radicals and a murder method that was sensationally bloody.

Not only was there overwhelming physical evidence at the scene that Norbert had committed the crime, also he had been apprehended close by, his clothes drenched in blood. Dana Wright, to whom the entire family estate now came, paid for the very best Queen's Counsel that money could buy. Norbert was advised to plead not guilty by reason of insanity. Psychiatrists speaking for the prosecution declared that he was sane at the time of the murders; an opposing group for the defense declared vehemently that the accused was clearly demented.

If I'd been on the jury, I think I would have agreed with the latter opinion. Looking at Norbert's chiseled features and delightful smile, then at the photos showing the almost unbelievable ferocity of his attack upon his parents and sister, madness seemed the only explanation.

My mind leapt to the assignment ahead of me. Norbert had insanity as an excuse — the people with whom I shortly would be training had no such exoneration. They were eager to learn the most efficient methods of exterminating fellow humans — strangers who were categorized as "the enemy."

These acts of violence would be justified because

they were driven by philosophical or political beliefs. Assassination, destruction of water or power supplies, the sickness or death of thousands, perhaps hundreds of thousands of people, all for a creed, a doctrine, an idea.

And they were judged sane, and Norbert mad?

Of course, I reminded myself, Norbert *was* mad, bad, and excessively dangerous to know. Even so, at some level the scope of his crime could be understood and grasped. Suburban terrorism against innocent targets was a different matter. What was the phrase I'd heard in a TV courtroom drama just the other night? *Depraved indifference to life.* That summed it up well.

CHAPTER THREE

Six weeks had been too short a preparation for this mission. My trainer said so out loud; Livia, I was sure, thought the same. Add to this the fact that there wasn't much intelligence information about the principal players in Edification, the shadowy group I was infiltrating, and that only two of the other terrorism students who would be training with me had been definitely identified. The location of the camp, designated by the letter *E*, was in a remote area of Australia, where I'd be far from help, should I need it, and now there was a possibility that I would be stalked by a homicidal brother.

I became aware that Livia was frowning at me. She had turned sideways on her regulation government chair and had folded herself into a neat package with her arms around her knees. She should have looked awkward in this pose, but of course, being Livia, it seemed entirely natural.

"You're sure you want to go ahead with this? You can back out, no problems. It's dangerous enough without any added complications."

"No way am I backing out," I said. I gave her my best high-wattage smile to hide the fact that I'd thought, just for a moment, that getting out was just what I wanted to do. "I'm not wasting all that work becoming the blasted woman to throw it all away at the last minute."

We sat without speaking for what seemed a long time. I could hear the echo of my bold words, and wondered if Livia thought I'd spoken out of bravado or conviction. I broke the silence, saying, "And you have to admit we'll never get an opportunity quite like this again. I'll be in the belly of the organization." I threw my hands up. "Bam! We can blow it open from the inside out."

The corners of Livia's lips twitched. "Colorful," she said. "And if you run into Norbert?"

"I'll take him out, just like that," I said facetiously.

"Yes, do." Her tone was businesslike.

"You're telling me to kill him?" This was hardly standard ASIO practice, although a clear and imminent threat to one's life was grounds to use deadly force.

"This guy won't give you a second chance. Don't

stop to chat — and remember, he can charm the birds from the trees."

"I'm charm proof," I announced, although that wasn't strictly true, because at the moment I was finding Livia's concern quite charming.

"We're probably worrying about nothing," said Livia. "His sister's had no contact with him since the trial, so he'll have a job finding out where she's gone."

Dana had attended court every day, but she hadn't visited Norbert in jail, nor had she made any attempt to see him once he was sentenced. After selling the Sussex house she moved to a small flat in London, continuing from that base the family tradition of support for far left-wing causes. Her hatred of the establishment was stronger than ever, and she told associates that she intended to become even more involved on the front lines.

As a matter of course Dana Wright had been of interest to British security, especially as she was virulently opposed to the very concept of hereditary rulers, and had categorized the royal family, in one of her milder moments, as "filthy, bloodsucking parasites growing fat on the body of the nation."

Telephone taps revealed that she was actively pursuing the idea of moving back to Australia, and to that end she had made close contact with various radical organizations in Sydney and Melbourne. This, of course, was of great interest to ASIO, particularly when ASIO broke a series of encrypted messages between Dana and a shadowy group based in Sydney calling itself, with a surprising touch of humor, Edification.

The evidence was that Edification was developing terrorist training camps patterned along the lines of

17

the very effective jihad camps in Afghanistan, where Islamic extremists were taught the skills to launch bloody attacks on western targets.

Edification, however, had taken this concept and made it nonexclusionary, with only two requirements for potential students: first, that each person be a genuine extremist with a curriculum vitae containing well-documented proof of radical beliefs and actions; second, that each person make the payment of a considerable sum of money in American dollars in cash.

Dana Wright had no trouble with either of these requirements, and she was accepted for the next intake of students to be held at Camp E somewhere in the Kimberley region of northwest Australia.

Any attempts by ASIO to infiltrate Edification had been unsuccessful, and they had only second- and third-hand evidence of the organization's activities, and no definite location of the training site. The group remained an elusive but very real threat to Australia's security, so Dana Wright's involvement became the focus of intense interest.

Shortly after finalizing attendance details, Dana made a fateful decision. She was, I had been resigned to discover, keen on extreme physical challenges, and six weeks before Edification's training was to begin, she had taken an unscheduled break and had set off for a solo rock-climbing trip in Scotland.

She was under security surveillance when she fell while trying to negotiate a fearsome cliff, sustaining serious head injuries. The British security agents watching seized the opportunity the accident offered, accompanying Dana's unconscious body to the nearest emergency department, then arranging for her to be admitted to an upscale private hospital under the same phony name they'd given when she had first been treated.

No one came looking for her. Since the murders she'd become very much a loner, often disappearing overseas for weeks at a time, and the story was discreetly circulated among her associates that Dana was on some clandestine mission.

Her flat was covertly searched, and everything that could assist the planting of a substitute was taken and copied. After a blizzard of communications between British and Australian authorities, I was told I'd been selected to become Dana Wright. I was a little taller, but we were about the same weight and build, both of us had blondish hair and were approximately the same age. Dana had blue eyes, and mine were indeterminate hazel, but as I wore contacts, all I had to do was switch to blue-tinted lenses.

It was fortunate that because of her family's background in activism, Dana had always been scrupulous about avoiding media photographs, and she'd never been interviewed on television, so the only clear images of her, apart from family albums, would be official ones such as appeared on her driver's license or in her passport, and we had those covered.

Although she'd been mobbed each time she appeared at court for her brother's trial, she had always worn dark glasses and a concealing scarf around her head. She had been a witness for the prosecution, and it was helpful that British courts did not allow the media to photograph or videotape proceedings, so the only representation of Dana Wright from the trial was a sketch by a press artist.

So, while Dana Wright lay comatose under a false name in a hospital in southern Scotland, I was doing a crash course in becoming her. This preparation included studying everything about her family background, learning her personal habits and idiosyncrasies, making sure I knew the geography and street names of any place with which she might be expected to be familiar, memorizing details of what seemed thousands of radical groups she'd been in contact with, and because of her interest in punishing physical exercise — the woman ran marathons, for pity's sake! — getting mega-fit myself.

Livia checked her watch, unfolded herself smoothly, and stood up. "You better get moving. I'll send someone to collect you." She bit her lip, then said, "Denise, be careful." She'd used my real name on purpose this time.

Being careful was high on my to-do list. For the first time in my undercover career I'd have absolutely no backup. If I got into trouble in the middle of nowhere, I would have to get myself out of it. Both of us knew that I would be summarily executed if my true identity got out.

"One thing," I said, "am I supposed to know my brother's escaped?"

"It only happened a few hours ago, and the British media's just picked up on it. The wire services will take it international, but right now the only way you could know is if you had a call from London from a friend, or a journalist tracked you down. Do you want me to set something up?"

I shook my head. "It's better if it comes as a great big shock to me."

At the door, Livia said, "I hope to hear from you at least once before you leave Sydney." She gave me a small smile. "Good luck."

Five minutes later the same guy who'd dropped me off at the room turned up and took me back to the immigration processing area, which was even more crowded than before. He cleared me through himself, but I was on my own from then on. As I waited in yet another queue I thought of what I'd do, remote chance though it was, if Norbert turned up.

The trail of flights and accommodations that had been constructed for the fictional Dana Wright was convincing, but if the time ever came that Norbert Cummins saw me face to face, he'd know at once that I wasn't his younger sister.

I wondered, if I were Norbert, what I'd do in that situation. Say, "You're not my sister. Oh, well . . ." and walk off. Or kill me anyway?

Given he had nothing to lose, and was a certified lunatic anyway, I guessed he'd kill me, right there and then. Unless I got him first.

CHAPTER FOUR

The office of TrekTrak Ecology Tours was located in an unprepossessing little shop front on Parramatta Road in the inner city suburb of Annandale. Traffic thundered by, exhaust fumes scented the air, and someone had dumped the detritus from a fast-food meal next to the front door. There were a few curled-edge posters stuck in the window featuring sun-faded shots of bushland, native flora and fauna, and water with many birds lifting off from a lagoon in some anonymous national park.

Inside wasn't much of an improvement. There

were no computer terminals, usually ubiquitous in travel agencies, just three bare metal desks, and one at the front with a few travel leaflets spread over its surface and what appeared to be the only telephone in the place.

This desk was also occupied by a young guy who looked about seventeen. He had a pimply face and one of the most prominent Adam's apples I'd ever seen. His white T-shirt was rather grubby, and he wore an elaborate chrome watch with many dials that looked ludicrous on his skinny wrist.

TrekTrak Ecology Tours was the front Edification used to disguise the real purpose of the organization. Having it as a tour agency gave the added advantage that clients could be transported to the Kimberley region posing as genuine ecotourists. This way the arrival of a bunch of disparate people in such a sparsely settled area wouldn't arouse suspicions, although frankly I'd have to say personally I'd be suspicious of anyone who booked a trip to anywhere with this outfit.

"Yeah?" said the young man, reluctantly tearing his gaze from a girlie magazine. Even from my vantage point I could only marvel at the size and shape of the buoyant breasts on the sultry-positioned naked female bodies.

"Implants," I said — or rather, Dana said. I knew from my research that Dana Wright wouldn't let something like that pass without comment. She would have snapped the word out with scorn, but my tone was helpful, rather than condemnatory.

"What?"

I jerked my head in the direction of his magazine. "Not a genuine breast in the bunch of them. Silicone, saline, whatever. You don't think unenhanced women look like that, do you?"

He slapped the magazine shut. "Look, what do you want?" He swallowed, and I watched with fascination as his Adam's apple bobbed. "If you're selling something, you're wasting your time."

"I'm booked on the next TrekTrak tour."

"Yeah?" There was a minimal sharpening of interest. "What's your name?"

"Dana Wright."

He slid open the top drawer and consulted something. "Got identification?"

I dug out my passport and handed it to him. "This do?"

He looked at the photo, sniggered, then looked at me. "You look like you carked it."

"I'm very much alive," I said, "and I want to see whoever's in charge." He opened his mouth, but I spoke first. "And that's not *you*, mate."

The person in charge turned out to be a woman who had been summoned by a telephone call from Howie — I'd got his name when he said into the receiver, "Howie here. Another one's arrived. You'd better come round."

Ten minutes later a woman in jeans and a bright coral top came though the door smiling. "You must be Dana! It's wonderful to have you on board!"

It was only when I felt my shoulders relax a little that I realized how tense I'd been about this first contact with Edification.

I said, "And you are?"

"Oh, how rude of me." She stuck out her hand. "Brit Talbertson. I'm your" — she broke off to tilt her head and wink at me meaningfully with one baby blue — "I'm your tour guide. We'll be seeing a lot of each other in the next few weeks."

Her handshake was almost too firm. She released my fingers, saying, "I'm sure that you realize this is just a formality, but may I see your passport and driver's license, please?"

I would have been astonished if she hadn't asked for at least two items of identification. I expected some pointed questions, too. Handing her my passport, I said, "Howie's already remarked that my photo makes me look like a corpse."

Howie wasn't listening. I could see he was itching to get back to his girlie magazine, but didn't dare to do so while Brit Talbertson was there.

Brit laughed sympathetically as she viewed my passport. "That's not so bad!" she exclaimed. "You should see mine."

She checked my British driver's license with care, then said, "You have more than one passport, don't you?"

"That's right." As Dana Wright's father had been born in England, his children were entitled to British passports. I unzipped the inside pocket of my shoulder bag to retrieve it. "Much better photo in this one. I use it to get in and out of Britain and when I visit the Continent. Otherwise I use my Aussie passport."

She leafed through it, checking the entry and exit stamps, then, smiling, handed it back. "I'm so pleased you don't mind my checking — but you must understand for security reasons we have to be very careful."

"Wouldn't have it any other way."

Her smile was replaced with a look of concern. "I know you flew in first thing this morning from the States, Dana. I hope you don't suffer too much from jet lag, because we'll be leaving late this afternoon. We're booked on a flight to Darwin."

The fact that she knew that I'd entered the country this Friday morning was no worry, as an e-mail, ostensibly from Dana Wright, had been sent to TrekTrak giving travel details, but the tour departure this afternoon wasn't on the schedule.

"Today?" I said, lifting my eyebrows with surprise. "I thought we left on Monday."

This was a complication: I'd hoped to get in at least one call to Livia about my first contacts. The intelligence information on Edification was so sparse that only a few of the players had been identified, and even in those cases there wasn't much available, so anything I could relay would be a help.

"I'm so sorry if it's inconvenient," Brit said, her face now rueful, "but it's a necessary change. Your luggage?"

"At my hotel."

"Ah!" Brit flashed me the warmest of smiles. "You can give me your key and hotel details, and I'll arrange for someone to pick up your things for you."

I shook off the ripple of uneasiness I felt at the change of plans. "It's no trouble, Brit. I'm traveling light, of course, so it'll only take me a moment or two to get everything together."

"No, I insist." Now she was solicitous. "You're to relax and let me look after everything." Another smile. Brit's teeth, I decided, had all been capped, they were so perfect. "You'll be extended enough when we reach our destination."

She took my arm companionably. "I do hope you've had time for a hot shower. International travel is so" — she made a graceful gesture with her free hand — "cooped up in a metal tube with all those people."

Brit's identity was as much a fabrication as mine. She might well be as Australian as she sounded, but no one of that name had been born where she claimed, nor was her degree in tourism genuine. The briefing photograph I'd seen was a pale reflection of Brit Talbertson in the flesh. Popping with energy, radiating enthusiasm in almost palpable waves, she was one of those people whose first meeting would be impossible to forget. She had glossy brown hair, extraordinary amber eyes, a full mouth, and a set of facile expressions and gestures that seemed too glibly appropriate. And she smiled too much.

In short, she irritated the hell out of me.

Howie didn't seem to be a fan either. He glowered when Brit snapped her fingers at him. "Howie, the list. And you can close up now."

He took a piece of paper from the top drawer of the desk and handed it to her. "You said I'd get extra for this arvo."

A frown of displeasure creased Brit's forehead. "It's barely one o'clock. You can hardly say you've been on duty the whole afternoon."

He pushed out his bottom lip. "You said I'd get extra."

She released my arm to fish in the hip pocket of her jeans. "Very well."

He counted the money carefully while Brit watched him with false patience. Satisfied, he said, "Okay, I'll lock up, then."

She pointed to a mail slot set into the bottom of the front door. "After you do, put the key through there, right?"

"Yeah."

Outside in the street, she shook her head with apparent wonder. "How *do* they ever get a job, let alone keep it?"

"He's got a job with TrekTrak," I pointed out.

"Just casual work for a couple of days. Howie's out of work, as of now." Brit gave me a conspiratorial grimace. "He knows nothing, of course."

"Of course."

I'd assumed she'd arrived in a car, but Brit set out walking at a brisk pace. She wasn't an amateur. As we made our way around the corner and into a side street I noticed her checking everything around her — passing traffic, parked vehicles, anyone else on foot. Although I hadn't been informed — sometimes ignorance kept one from making stupid mistakes — I assumed that ASIO had us under surveillance. Fortunately Brit didn't detect any evidence of this, and neither did I.

There was one piece of advice I could have given her: don't wear brightly colored clothes — your coral top can be seen for some distance. Neutral shades are best.

"I suppose, living in London, you know Leonard Ouster well," Brit said. "I believe he's very active in protesting the American military presence in Europe."

I could swear there was no Leonard Ouster in Dana Wright's contacts, nor was the name mentioned in any of the lists I'd studied so assiduously. "Leonard Ouster?" I said. "I'm afraid I don't know him. Are you sure you've got the right name?"

Brit looked at me with polite surprise. "You don't recognize his name?"

This was a test. If I waffled now, she'd be on me like a shot, sure that something was wrong. "Never heard of him," I said. "Now, I *do* know Chris Chatley. Bit long in the tooth — she'd be seventy-five if she's a day — but a powerhouse in Ban Uncle Sam, which is the organization I think you must mean."

It would almost be a pleasure to ramble on with more details, as my brain was stuffed with them, but my ASIO trainer had at last drummed into me that embroidering with unnecessary facts was suspicious in itself.

Brit shook her head. "You're right. I've got the names mixed up. Leonard's active in the States, not in Britain."

"I've still never heard of him," I said. "He can't be that active."

Brit smiled. "My mistake."

Away from the main road the streets rapidly became residential. We came to a narrow alley and she ducked into it, hurrying along the potholed surface until we came out onto another street.

"I'm the last to arrive then, am I?"

She turned her head sharply, forgetting to smile. "The last? What makes you think that?"

"Hey, it's not so hard to work out. Howie had a list of names, which means there was more than just me, and when he called you, he announced that I was another one, which indicates that at least one person had arrived before me. Then, when we left, you told him to close up. And outside, you said Howie was out of work now." I grinned at her. "I'm a regular Sherlock Holmes, eh?"

"I'm impressed, Dana. And you're right. One yesterday, one early this morning. Three more will join us in Darwin, and the rest will already be there when we arrive at E."

Brit's smile was back. I wondered, uncharitably, if she smiled in her sleep. Chances were, she did. I hoped I never had any reason to find out for sure.

Half a block later, we dived into another narrow way running behind a row of houses. When we came to a dilapidated gate set into an equally neglected paling fence, she grabbed my hand. "In here." Her fingers gripped me tightly, and I had to beat down an impulse to shake her off.

"A bit cloak-and-dagger, isn't it?"

She frowned at me, then her face cleared. "You're joking."

I shrugged. "Nervous habit."

Nothing I'd read about Dana Wright indicated she found anything humorous, but this wasn't the type of information that went into written records unless the person was a standup comic, or renowned for making jokes.

Disentangling my hand from hers when she tapped on the blistered paint of the back door, I glared at the back of her shapely neck. Brit Talbertson was giving every evidence of being a touchy-feely type, and that was going to get tiresome. Not that I minded being touched in certain situations, but, attractive though she was, I couldn't see myself ever giving a warm reception to this chronic fingerer.

The door opened abruptly. A man stood aside and ushered us into the kitchen, which was shabby and old-fashioned, with a truly hideous Laminex table and matching green chairs. The room was full of the smell of coffee and cinnamon buns.

"Have you had lunch?" he asked me. "Or will coffee and a bun do?"

"Coffee, please. And a cinnamon bun would be great."

"This is Konrad," said Brit with an effervescent smile. "Konrad, meet Dana."

He nodded hello. "Black okay?"

"Thanks."

"Make yourself at home," said Brit, looking hospitable. "Oh, and Dana — from now on we only use first names. We don't want any of our clients embarrassed by a recognizable last name. I'm sure you'll understand."

"Sure."

I pulled out one of the ugly chairs and sank down on it. The combination of trans-Pacific jet lag plus being keyed up about my role as Dana Wright made everything around me feel not quite real. I smothered a yawn, then sharpened my wandering wits by assessing Konrad as he poured the brewed coffee from a battered silver coffeepot.

I knew his full name, Konrad Archer, but not because of an intelligence briefing. His name appeared on all the tour leaflets and confirmation e-mails that Dana had had in her London flat. Konrad Archer was the co-owner of TrekTrak with an O. P. Smith, who seemed not to exist. As far as the world was concerned, Konrad was the proprietor of the little TrekTrak ecology tour company, specializing in small-group excursions to remote Australian outback areas.

Out of habit, I mentally ran through how I would

describe him: above average height, medium build, thinning brown hair worn very short, a wide, mobile mouth, nose that had been broken at least once, what looked like permanently swollen knuckles. A boxer? Martial arts expert? He had a purple-and-red tattoo on the back of his left hand, the head of a snake, the sinuous body of which wound around his wrist and disappeared up under the sleeve of his dark blue shirt.

As he set a plate of hot buns in front of my now-watering mouth, Brit patted my shoulder. "I'll send Joyce to pick up your things, so you just sit down and relax. Did you make any phone calls? She'll use a TrekTrak credit card and cover them, along with the cost of the room."

My answer wouldn't make any difference. Joyce, whoever she was, would check anyway if I'd made any calls, and then she'd go through my luggage with a fine-tooth comb. She wouldn't find anything untoward. Every item had been checked and rechecked. My suitcase had been bought in the U.K., the clothes had British labels, the toiletries had been purchased in London stores, as had the heavy-duty walking boots — boots that I'd spent some time wearing to break them in so they didn't look too new. My underclothes were from Marks & Spencer and, in a nice touch, every item in a plastic bag containing chocolate bars and sweets indicated that they'd been manufactured in Britain.

"Don't I know you?"

The American-accented voice came booming from the inner entrance to the kitchen. I looked up from my coffee, outwardly calm, but inwardly quailing. It was my worst nightmare to have one of the unknown students turn out to be someone who knew Dana Wright in person.

The speaker was a shortish, compact man with broad shoulders and large hands. He had a tanned, pleasant face, with deep creases bracketing his mouth, and heavy sandy eyebrows matching his fair, sun-bleached hair.

"I'm sorry?" I said, seeming puzzled. I was very conscious that Konrad and Brit were watching me.

The man came striding over, a grin on his face. He had on a khaki shirt and trousers, and he shook my hand with a ferocious pressure. " 'Don't I know you?' is what I said, but I don't — at least, not yet. I have to confess it's my pickup line. Has it worked?"

"Startlingly successful," I said. "I'm yours. More or less."

"Call me Fergus. Means 'strong man' in Gaelic. Don't imagine you knew that."

"I'm Dana." Pleased that I had the opportunity to use something esoteric I'd looked up, I added, "It means 'from Denmark.' "

"But you're not, are you?" He cocked his head. "English? I'm very good with accents."

After all the trouble I'd taken in perfecting an Aussie accent with English overtones, this was very annoying. Before I could set him straight, Brit said severely, "We don't discuss countries of origin or any background information."

"Hell, Brit, you've stymied all my small talk!"

My small talk was stymied by something else. I had the compelling feeling that even if this guy didn't know me, I knew *him*. I couldn't remember where or when we'd met — if we had. Perhaps I'd seen a photograph of him somewhere...

The memory danced just out of reach. I devoutly hoped I'd catch it before we left civilization and I was beyond help if I needed it.

CHAPTER FIVE

"Hey, Konrad, I could do with a coffee." Fergus stood waiting, it seemed, for Konrad to get it for him.

Konrad indicated the coffeepot. "Help yourself."

From his offhand tone and the expression on his face, I got the impression that Konrad actively disliked Fergus, a fact that was worth noting. In the days ahead I had to be hypersensitive to the relationships that would develop in an isolated camp. Accurately reading the subtleties of likes and dislikes, of animosity versus friendship, would give me an edge that I might need to survive.

Fergus got his coffee, then pulled up a chair beside me, gearing up, I feared, for a friendly conversation. I was planning strategies to avoid this, as my eyes were drooping and I was fighting to keep some semblance of alertness.

I smothered yet another yawn, murmured "Jet lag" as an explanation, and was about to ask Brit if there was somewhere I could rest for an hour or so, when Fergus, cradling his mug in his large, square hands, said, "Don't tell me you came in from London today! Brutal! Done it myself several times, and twenty-four hours or more in a plane is no joke."

"I flew in from Los Angeles."

"From L.A.? Know it well." He inclined toward me, his tone confidential. "My group — we did a dry run at LAX. One of the busiest airports in the country, you know."

"Dry run?"

"Just a feasibility study. Seven separate terminals, with seven separate bombs going off simultaneously..." He leaned back, obviously picturing the satisfying results. "You know how many people go through LAX every day? It'd be pandemonium. Tie up the fire service, the cops, overwhelm the hospitals. Then we hit our next target..."

"Ambitious," I said, with a moderately appreciative look. Inwardly I was repelled that dealing out death and destruction could be discussed so cheerfully, although at the training camp I knew that I, too, would be talking with the same enthusiasm about mounting similar terrorist attacks.

"That's why I'm here," declared Fergus, smiling at Konrad and Brit. "My dad always said that if a job's worth doing, it's worth doing well. Edification's going to give me all the logistics and technical information to carry out the mission with total success."

I didn't ask who his group was — that would have been far too inquisitive in this world where secrets were the stock in trade. However, in the days ahead I was aiming to become a friendly comrade for Fergus so I could gradually milk him for details that would help identify his organization.

"Speaking of success," said Fergus, swinging around in his chair, "were those fires in the Melbourne abortion clinics set by one of your graduates?"

Konrad and Brit spoke simultaneously, Konrad saying, "No comment," and Brit exclaiming, "Yes!"

"That's great," said Fergus. "Confirms the rumor I heard." Giving Konrad a disparaging look, he went on, "I don't know why you're so tight-assed about it. It's great publicity for you. You need to take a constructive look at the PR angle."

As he continued to expand on his ideas of what Edification should be doing to build a solid reputation as a terrorist resource, I watched Konrad's body language. Personally, I wouldn't have continued giving advice if I'd been Fergus. Konrad's wide mouth was a tight line of anger, his eyes were narrowed, and his stance was classic en garde — chin down to protect his throat, his weight balanced, one foot a little forward, knees slightly bent, his elbows tucked in, his hands in front of him, ready to strike.

Brit bit her lip, looking from one to the other. Perhaps, I thought, Brit had witnessed Konrad losing it before, in similar circumstances.

When Fergus paused, a cocky aren't-I-smart look on his face, Brit, in a patent attempt to change the subject, said urgently to Konrad, "Joyce is late. I hope nothing's happened. She should be back with Mokhtar by now."

As if on command, the slam of what I presumed was the front door reverberated.

Obviously relieved at the interruption, Brit exclaimed, "Ah, there she is!"

After a moment a woman appeared to stare at me inquisitively. She was middle-aged and rather drab, apart for a fanatical gleam in her black eyes. She was thin to the point of being gaunt, and her dark, gray-streaked hair was pulled back in an unflattering pony-tail. Behind her was a slight young man with black hair and olive skin.

"Dana, this is Joyce," said Brit, in full introduction mode. "And with her is Mokhtar. Joyce, this is —"

"I get the picture," snapped Joyce. To me she said, "You've heard about your brother? I just caught it on the car radio."

As I was Dana Wright learning this disturbing news for the first time, I decided on an attitude of mild astonishment. Although Dana had every reason to hate her brother for what he'd done, she was far too controlled, I thought, to blurt out something like, "I hope the bastard's dead!" so I said, "On the radio? My brother? What's happened?"

Joyce had the keenly delighted expression of one who enjoys breaking bad news. "Escaped from the loony bin," she announced.

Mokhtar's expression didn't change, but the others showed various levels of surprise.

Brit, whose face predictably had shown the strongest response — blue eyes wide and jaw dropping — recovered to say severely, "Joyce, please remember we don't share personal information."

Ignoring this, Joyce went on. "He killed some doctor and got clear away."

Livia had said the psychiatrist had been savagely beaten, not killed, so either the news source was wrong, or Joyce had misheard. "Norbert killed someone?"

"Bashed him," said Joyce, nodding. "Took his clothes as a disguise and walked through all the security gates. No one even tried to stop him."

Brit, obviously giving up any attempt to stop Joyce from mining this forbidden area of personal information, shook her head. "Dreadful," she commented to the room in general. "Just dreadful."

How sweet, I thought. Here she is commiserating over the escape of psychotic Norbert Cummins, when she promotes with cool equanimity the murdering of any number of innocents by terrorists.

"Your brother's insane?" asked Fergus, his face alive with curiosity. Clearly he wouldn't win a prize for diplomacy.

"I'm afraid so."

"Tough."

Mokhtar, moving with almost feline grace, came into the center of the room. "Is any of this of importance?" he asked in a light, subtly accented voice. "Something happening in one's personal life is of no relevance to the rest of us, is it?"

Brit shot him an irritated glance, then put a hand on my arm. "Dana, you must be so upset. Is there someone you want to call? Please — treat everything here as yours."

It seemed appropriate at this point to inject some raw emotion into my response. "I don't want to call anyone," I said with a controlled venom, removing my

arm from her clasp. "Norbert destroyed my family —
those I was closest to in the world." I allowed myself
a dramatic pause. "There's no one left I'd want to
ring."

"Oh, dear," said Brit. I could almost believe her
eyes had a sheen of tears. "That's so sad — not to
have someone to call at a moment of personal need."

Joyce gave an unexpected cackle of laughter. "So
who'd *you* call, Brit? Siobhan?"

For a moment Brit looked taken aback, then her
face darkened. "Shut up, Joyce!"

Konrad's face had a matching scowl. "Yes, shut the
hell up, Joyce," he ground out.

Unfazed, Joyce said, "If you can't take the
heat . . ." She gave another harsh chuckle as she made
a sweeping gesture to indicate the room. "Then like
they say, get out of the kitchen."

I took a sip of the excellent coffee, then a large
bite of cinnamon bun. I had no idea who Siobhan
might be, but I was looking forward to meeting her.

CHAPTER SIX

Waiting at the airport, which to my bleary eyes looked pretty much like any other terminal the world over, I puzzled over why Edification hadn't searched my shoulder bag, the clothes I wore and, for that matter, my body.

Deep in conversation, Konrad, Brit, and Joyce were standing together some distance away. To me Konrad looked dangerous in a break-your-bones sort of way, but that could have been the effect his broken nose and callused knuckles had upon me. Being tall, he inclined his head toward the women, but there was no deference in his body language. My eyes were drawn to the snake head on the back of his hand. I wondered if the body of the reptile encircled his arm all the way up, as though the ink were a python, ready to crush his flesh.

Joyce, her thin frame erect, was listening closely. Every now and then she interposed, and the others paid close attention to her words.

Brit, for once her animated smile not in evidence, was very vocal, glancing frequently to where Fergus, Mokhtar, and I sat. Her face, usually so expressive, was almost devoid of expression.

The chain of command was still a puzzle to me. ASIO hadn't been able to establish whether Edification was run by committee, or if there was a designated leader or leaders. Meeting Konrad, I'd thought that he, being the front man for TrekTrak and having a formidable physical presence, might head the organization, but now I wasn't so sure. It was always possible that the boss of the outfit had no apparent connection with Edification, and ruled, as it were, from afar. Or that he, or she, was at Camp E.

Giving up on this speculation, I listened to Mokhtar and Fergus having a desultory conversation about recent developments in security devices at airports, and the most expedient ways to circumvent them. This got me thinking about spy equipment in general.

Any of us three could be carrying miniature recording devices, cameras, or, probably more to the point, an electronic beacon that could be picked up by the Global Positioning System's satellites.

GPS technology was so exact that it was being used in California to monitor minute movements of the Earth's crust that might predict a coming earthquake, so a signal sent from wherever we ended up in the wilds of northern Australia could pinpoint Edification's Camp E precisely.

As I had prepared for the assignment Livia and I had discussed whether or not to outfit me with the latest technology, especially as items could now be so easily hidden, with cameras concealed in shirt buttons, tiny video cameras set into a wristwatch, and minute hearing aids that could pick up voices well out of normal range.

"The reason they haven't been infiltrated is that they're super careful," I had said. "Besides, if they catch me with something that makes me look like a latter-day James Bond, I'd say my cover would be well and truly blown."

I remembered that at that point I'd grinned at her, and asked if a poison capsule attached to one of my back molars would be included in the kit. Livia hadn't laughed, observing coolly that if I were discovered, torture during interrogation was a likely scenario before they dispatched me. That had wiped the smile off my face.

The final judgment had been that I'd carry nothing that could possibly incriminate me, but still it nagged at me that this may have been the wrong decision.

I became aware that someone was standing over me. "Hey, Dana," said Fergus, hanging his sandy head in a mock humble manner, "I've come to beg a favor."

"And that is?"

"Sit next to me on the plane." He glanced over at Mokhtar, who was leafing through a magazine without much interest. "Right now I've got Mokhtar for the flight, and he's no live wire."

I forced an apologetic smile. "Sorry, Fergus, I fail the live wire test too. I plan to go to sleep as soon as we take off."

"Oh, come on! We can have a few drinks, a few laughs." When I shook my head he looked flatteringly disappointed. "Rain check, then?" he said.

I said, "Of course," reminding myself that I needed to stay on friendly terms with Fergus if I were to find out more about his LAX-bombing group.

The flight to Darwin, the capital of the Northern Territory and the largest city in Australia's far north, was uneventful. I dozed as much as possible, helped by the fact that Joyce, who was sitting beside me, said only a few words during the entire journey. Every time I woke she was in the same position — fingers linked on her lap, eyes open, contemplating the back of the seat in front of her. It was quite unnerving, this quiet, blank stare, but not enough to keep me awake.

I roused myself when the engine note changed, indicating we were coming into Darwin. The plane landed, taxied for ages, and the moment it came to a stop people leapt to their feet to get possessions from the overhead bins with such alacrity that one would have supposed we'd all be running from the aircraft in the next few moments. Naturally this was followed by an interminable wait with most passengers standing clutching their belongings, and a few slightly smug nonconformists still sitting down.

Generally I was one of the ready-to-run crowd, but

this time exhaustion kept me seated with Joyce, who seemed quite content to let the plane clear before she moved.

Brit, who'd been out of her seat belt and getting her things even before the FASTEN SEAT BELT sign went out, squeezed her way through the crush so she could mother-hen over us. "I think you better get ready to go. We'll be getting off the plane any moment now. I mean, we have to collect luggage and get taxis..."

I nodded politely. Joyce's lip lifted in a sneer.

The plane emptied, Joyce and I collected our things and were among the last to come out into the bright lights of yet another airport lounge. Brit, jigging impatiently next to the others, gestured to us to hurry.

"What do you think of her?" said Joyce, unexpectedly.

"Who? Brit?"

"Yes. Brit."

"Well," I said, playing for time, "I hardly know her..."

Joyce waited.

"I think she'd be easy to underestimate."

A slight nod. "Good answer," Joyce said.

Darwin was new to me, but I wasn't likely to recognize it if I went there again, because it was dark when we arrived and Brit informed us all that we would be spending some hours at a nearby motel, and that it would still be dark when we left on a small charter plane very early the next morning.

Outside the terminal the roads were slick with

water. The hot, moist air reminded me that up here in the North it was still the tail end of the wet season, which ran December to March. Livia and I had discussed why Edification wouldn't wait until at least April, when the Dry began. Our best guess was that it was because the Wet attracted far less tourists. "And," Livia had said, "part of your training may be to rough it by having you up to your knees in water and leeches." She'd laughed at my expression.

We needed two taxis to fit in everybody plus their luggage. I was in the first vehicle with Konrad, Joyce, and Mokhtar, and as Dana Wright had never shown signs of being a pushover who could be shunted from place to place without complaint, I took the opportunity to grumble about being squashed in the back between Mokhtar and Joyce, and threw in a few acerbic comments about the inconvenience of being forced onto another aircraft almost immediately after arriving in Sydney seriously jet-lagged.

No one made any attempt to soothe my ruffled feathers, but Konrad did comment that I'd be able to grab a few hours' sleep at the motel before we left for Kununurra.

My complaints ceased as I mulled this over. I'd studied maps of Northern Australia until my eyes had crossed, and I knew Kununurra, around seven hundred kilometers from Darwin, was regarded as the eastern gateway to the Kimberley region. The town had been developed in the nineteen-sixties to support the huge Ord River Irrigation Project, and was situated near the artificially created Lake Argyle, one thousand square kilometers of water and home to a large variety of birdlife. Kununurra was also near the

Mirima National Park, and the Argyle Diamond Mine, where the rare Argyle Pink Diamond . . .

I grinned to myself: if all else failed, I could take a job as a tourist guide.

Another useful item of tourist information popped into my mind — the Ibis Aerial Highway. Because of the distances and the difficulty of access by road in the Kimberleys, a whole system of airstrips for light aircraft had been established, often on private land, so it was possible to fly direct to various locations in a fraction of the time it would take by road.

"Do we pick up another little plane at Kuna . . . Kuna . . ."

"Kununurra." Konrad completed my sentence for me. "No. We'll be in four-wheel drives from then on."

That might mean that Camp E was relatively close by. It didn't seem all that likely, though, as the area was probably the most popular tourist destination for the region.

When we clambered out of the taxi at the plain little motel I said to Konrad, "Are we meeting the others here? Brit said we would."

"Did she?" Konrad cast a frowning glance at Brit, who had just climbed out of the second taxi. "What else did she say?"

I shrugged. "Nothing I remember." He started to turn away, and I grabbed at his elbow. "Well?" I said, as pushy as I trusted Dana would have been. "After all, we're going to be spending the next weeks together, and I'm interested to meet them."

This wasn't my gregarious nature coming to the fore, but rather self-interest. Darwin was getting close to the final abort opportunity. ASIO would still have our party under surveillance, so that if one of the three joining us here in Darwin turned out to know Dana Wright personally, or recognized me in my real identity as Denise Cleever, I could bail out. Later, when we were deep in wild bushland, it would be a much dicier proposition.

Konrad checked his watch. "Everyone needs to hear this," he said to me. Raising his voice, he announced to the knot of people clustered around the taxis, "General meeting in twenty minutes in room eight. Leave all your luggage here. You'll get it later. You have enough time to get your keys, go to your rooms, and freshen up."

My motel room was basic but clean. I put down my things and looked around. A print of a black swan serenely floating on a river was the sole decoration on the beige walls. I frowned. I hated beige as a matter of principle. The bedspread had a faded pink pattern, and a quick examination showed that the mattress was rather lumpy. There was no phone.

It was paranoid to think I was under surveillance at this point, but probably wise to assume it. I had a vision of Konrad, Brit, and Joyce scrabbling through the luggage in the motel's office, but surely twenty minutes wouldn't be enough time to check everything.

The clock radio had a crack in its plastic casing, but it worked. I tried several stations to see if I could pick up any information about Norbert, but I couldn't find anything but music or talk. Surely even here in the remote north of Australia the exploits of a British ax murderer — *hatchet* murder didn't seem quite so severe — would make the news.

Giving up, I explored the bathroom. The lighting

over the mirror was cruel. I made a face at my reflection, removed my contacts and put drops in my somewhat bloodshot eyes, washed my face, cleaned my teeth with the toothbrush kit I always kept in my shoulder bag, put my contacts back in, and checked my appearance in the mirror again. No improvement. I contemplated putting makeup on, but what the hell — I wasn't going to be wearing any in the bush, so everyone would have to get used to me unadorned.

Room eight was larger than mine, but the décor was identical, except that the print over the beds was of a heron taking off from silvered water. The room quickly filled up. There were four strangers, one of whom was with Edification, a husky guy named Vince with flat obsidian eyes and an almost lipless mouth. Our three fellow students were introduced as Patsy, Rob, and Tom.

Patsy was in her late forties, with a comfortably padded body, fine flyaway hair, and a hearty manner. Rob had a long face dominated by an unfortunate putty nose that drooped over his small mouth and pointed chin. The third one, Tom, was the most presentable, being young, fit, and smoothly cheerful, although I wasn't particularly taken with his luxuriant mustache, which was a shade darker than his copper hair.

I was pleased that I'd never seen any of them before, and not one said, "My God, Dana/Denise, what are you doing here!" so I figured I was safe for the moment.

Brit gave a graceful little speech welcoming everyone to the "tour" — she winked as she said this — and handed over to Konrad.

He didn't bother with niceties. After telling us we were not to leave the motel grounds, and that if we were hungry there were vending machines near the motel's office, he went on to say, "Each of you must submit to a full body search and examination of all your belongings. It's for security — both ours and yours. Any questions?"

There was silence, then a couple of remarks, both of them negative in content.

"What if we refuse?" Mokhtar's flawless skin was flushed, and his light voice had a whiplash tone. "We were told nothing of this . . . this invasion of our privacy."

Unmoved, Konrad said, "Anyone who refuses this practical security procedure will not continue in the course. This motel is as far as you will go."

He waited to see if Mokhtar would say anything more, and when he didn't turned to the rest of us. "Other comments? Okay, let's get this over with quickly. You will all wait here, then one at a time you will be escorted to your room where the search will take place. The women will be searched by Brit and Joyce, the men by Vince and myself."

"I'll go first," I said. I was tired and I wanted to lie down on my motel bed, no matter how lumpy it might be. If stripping was the way to get there faster, I was all for it.

CHAPTER SEVEN

Silently blessing Livia for agreeing to put the kibosh on electronic devices, I followed Joyce and Brit to retrieve my top-of-the-line soft-sided suitcase and overnight bag from the pile of luggage stacked in the motel office, which was being guarded by a thin young woman in a grubby orange sundress and flip-flops. "No one's touched nothin'," she volunteered, in between quick sucks at a cigarette.

"Who's she?" I asked once we were out of earshot.

Brit looked surprised at my question. "Why do you need to know?"

I beamed at her. "I wondered if she were a member of Edification, and if I'd be seeing more of her."

Joyce gave a snort of laughter. "Not bloody likely."

Taking my comment as a serious query, Brit said helpfully, "I believe her name is Cheryl. She works for the motel, not for us. We're paying her a few dollars to keep an eye on the luggage."

"She's joking, Brit," said Joyce.

Brit looked puzzled, then irritated. "Very funny," she said with a hurt look in my direction.

Laden with my suitcase and overnight bag, I led the way to my room, thinking that Edification procedures were smart. I knew everything had been searched by Joyce when she'd picked up my things from my Sydney hotel, and care had been taken to make sure I hadn't been left alone with them since, so they were still clean, as I'd had no opportunity to surreptitiously hide any device that I might be carrying with me.

When I got to my door I dumped everything on the floor and dug in my jeans pocket to find the key. Unlocking the door, I said, "Drugs? Is that what you expect to find?"

My question was ignored by Joyce, but Brit, with an expression nicely blending concern and determination, said, "Dana, I realize this is embarrassing, but we must make sure no one is smuggling in any sort of surveillance equipment. MI5, MI6, ASIO, the CIA — any of them could be trying to infiltrate Edification. It's for everyone's protection for us to make sure there are no devices like that being brought into Camp E."

I'd left the light on, and the little room seemed to be trying its best to look welcoming. Shutting the door firmly, I checked that it was locked, not intending that anyone else would have the chance of seeing me in the buff. "I want to put it on record," I announced, "that I strongly object to this. I paid a lot of money to be here. Why in hell would I sabotage the program?"

Her thin face impassive, Joyce didn't respond. Predictably, Brit did. "I'm afraid we'll have to ask you to take off all your clothes, Dana. I do hope you don't mind."

"Won't matter if Dana does." Joyce tipped the contents of my shoulder bag out onto the pink bedspread.

"I don't mind," I said, "as long as you're gentle."

Not having a highly developed sense of humor — I was wondering if she had one at all — Brit blinked at my jocular comment, but I saw the trace of a smile on Joyce's lips as she sorted through the contents of my bag.

At first I'd thought that Joyce was well down on the Edification pecking order because she'd been driving Mokhtar around — he'd arrived in Sydney with, of all things, a toothache, and she'd taken him for emergency dental treatment — and then she'd gone off to collect my luggage from my hotel. Now I wasn't so sure.

Her relationship with Brit was at least that of an equal, and if she showed Konrad slightly more deference, it was probably because he didn't rub her the wrong way, as Brit obviously did.

Stepping out of my jeans, I sent a silent thank-you to the Good Sense Goddess who had obviously been hard at work the night some time ago when I'd been seriously tempted to have a small, tasteful dragon tattooed above my left ankle. Why a dragon? I couldn't quite remember, but it had seemed a good idea at the time. It was lucky that my ankle had remained pristine, as Dana Wright had no tattoos or birthmarks of any kind.

I glanced at Joyce, who was pawing through the contents of my bag. She was meticulous, examining every item closely. When I thought about it, this system of searching everyone once we were underway was another smart move. In Sydney I could have concealed some electronic device anywhere in the house, been searched, then retrieved it later. This way I had no opportunity to hide anything, unless... I glanced around the room, considering spots where I might have hidden something small.

"I'm going to have to ask you to please hurry," said Brit, properly regretful. "We have others to do, you see."

"Only one other," I pointed out. "And that's Patsy. Doesn't seem quite fair, does it? You have two, and the guys have four."

"It's admirable for you to worry about the division of labor," said Joyce, "but I'm sure they'll cope."

I repressed a grin. Joyce had made an unfavorable first impression on me, but I was beginning to appreciate her dry humor.

Unbuttoning my shirt, I heard the maddening buzz of a mosquito. "There's a mozzie in here!" I exclaimed. "And I'm the one providing the greatest expanse of skin."

Joyce ignored me. Brit turned her head trying to

locate the insect. "I come up in these awful red lumps if a mosquito bites me," she said. "It's a bitch."

"I imagine there are insects galore where we're going, and many of them much more dangerous than a mozzie."

Brit's shudder was genuine. "Jesus," she said, "I absolutely hate creepy-crawlies. And there're so many of them — spiders and snakes and centipedes half a meter long..."

"Get a grip, Brit!" Joyce snapped.

As I smiled at the near rhyme of "grip" and "Brit," the woman in question, plainly offended, busied herself with a close examination of my denim shirt. "I've got a microprocessor sewn into the collar," I said helpfully. Brit gave me a withering look.

"You wear contacts?" Joyce was holding the plastic container for my contact lenses. "You might have some trouble where we're going. It'll be hot and damp, and you'll have to be careful. You don't want eye problems in the middle of nowhere."

I was down to my underclothes. I unhooked my bra and handed it to Brit. In some circumstances a striptease could be sexy and fun, but this wasn't one of them. "I'm sure you searched my luggage, Joyce," I said, "so you know I've got a pair of specs with me. I can switch to them if I have to."

Joyce opened the case, which had two compartments. Frowning at my spare set of lenses, she said, "You wear tinted contacts?"

I gave her an abashed half-smile. "Call me shallow, but long ago I decided being blond wasn't enough. I wanted to be a blue-eyed blonde."

Joyce impressed me with her thoroughness by flipping open my passport. "Your passport says your eyes are blue."

"I know — I lied. Stupid to be conceited about it, I know, but everybody thinks I've got blue eyes."

My expression of chagrin showing how unjust I thought it was, I added, "If you want to know, my real color's sort of brownish-nothing. Anything would be an improvement."

Joyce looked at me thoughtfully, then went back to my shoulder bag, checking the inner seams carefully. Brit was examining my clothes in a similar fashion. I stood there, stark naked, thinking how hard it was to appear insouciant when all one had was bare skin to present to the world. I imagined nudists learned to take being undressed in front of strangers in their stride, but I felt at a serious disadvantage.

The mosquito made a coming-into-strike noise. I slapped the back of my neck. Missed. The mozzie went zinging away, triumphant.

"Hey, speed it up. I'm getting eaten alive here."

Joyce said, "Your bag's clean." She began to put everything back into it, which surprised me. She was the sort, I'd thought, who'd search in the manner of a customs department official — make a hell of a mess then leave the traveler to clean it up.

"This is all a bit rough, I must say." I was righteously indignant. "I'm coming here to learn how to terrorize others — not to be terrorized myself."

"I suspect it would be hard to terrorize you," said Joyce with a tight smile. "I've read your file."

For one sickening moment I thought that she knew I was Denise Cleever, then common sense told me that she must be referring to Dana Wright. It

seemed appropriate to give a modest shrug in acknowledgment of her comment.

When Brit indicated she'd found nothing, Joyce
handed me my clothes, pointed to a spot next to the
battered television set, and said, "Stand there. We
need to check the room."

So they *had* thought of everything. "You're
thorough," I commented in a tone of grudging admiration.

Because of the basic furnishings, the search for
possible hiding places took very little time. In place of
a wardrobe there was a curtained-off section containing a rail hung with bent wire hangers, and there
were no drawers, only open shelving. There wasn't
even a cupboard in the bathroom, just a shaky shelf
fixed to the wall by the basin.

"I was intending to get some sleep," I said, eyeing
the stripped bed and upside-down mattress. Joyce
removed the pillowcase and checked the pillow. "You'll
only have a couple of hours, anyway," she said unsym-
pathetically.

Five minutes later they were finished. At the door
Joyce paused, and for the first time she looked at me
with an appreciative expression. "You've got a good
body," she said. "I like that."

"Thanks," I said. "I think ..."

CHAPTER EIGHT

Awoken at an ungodly hour by Brit banging on the door and announcing we were leaving for the airport in forty minutes, I had a hasty, tepid shower with a minuscule cake of soap. I had finally murdered the sole mosquito in the room with a sharp slap, but its handiwork had left several itchy bumps. Fortunately I'd taken into account the medications I might need deep in tropical bushland and had included a large tube of ointment guaranteed to soothe the most irritating skin problem.

Dressed and packed in record time, I spent the last

few minutes fiddling with the clock radio, and at last was successful in raising a newscast.

Norbert's escape now had world attention, particularly because the young psychiatrist he had bashed — Joyce had been correct, he had suffered a fatal blood clot — had been revealed to be the only son of a beloved character actor, known for his roles in many movies. With this potent human interest angle to exploit, the media were in full cry.

By the end of the news item I knew that my "brother" was not on the run alone. Nellie Banks, one of the pack of adoring women who had formed Norbert's cheer squad at his trial, had been in touch with him while he was in captivity. From Norbert's point of view, Nellie was a gift from the gods, as she not only fancied herself in love with him, she was also a widow — a very rich widow. Once he had broken out of the asylum she provided both a luxurious refuge and access to large amounts of cash.

Now, romantically — from Nellie Banks's viewpoint — she and Norbert were fleeing from the law together, aided by her considerable financial resources. Police feared they had already left the country and were now on the Continent.

As the announcer went on to the next news — a beauty queen's arrest for inadvertently driving her Porsche into a crowd while high on cocaine — I sat on the edge of the bed and fought a queasy feeling in my stomach. True, my last meal had been airline food, but this nausea was caused by Norbert Cummins.

I told myself sternly this was totally ridiculous. Norbert had no way of knowing his sister's location. He didn't know about the real Dana lying in a Scottish hospital, and he wasn't aware that a fake

Dana was at this moment in a rundown Darwin motel in far-distant Australia.

Distant Australia. Even if he discovered Dana was supposed to be here, and heading for the Kimberleys, why would Norbert Cummins, with both the cops and the media hot on his trail, bother to travel half the world to find the remaining member of his family and kill her?

"Norbert," I said to empty air, "you'd have to be mad to take that risk."

And an answer came back, as if Norbert Cummins had materialized in the room and was speaking through me: *But isn't that what they've all been saying — I'm a psycho, a lunatic? Trust me, I have reasons for everything I do. You may not understand them, but they make perfect sense to me.*

Yawning in the predawn hush, we gathered beside the little ten-seater aircraft while our things were loaded. It seemed too fragile to fly seven hundred or so kilometers to the edge of the Kimberleys. To take my mind off the fragility of its wings and silver body, I checked who was present. No Tom.

"Where's Tom?" I said to Konrad, who was handing out brown paper bags euphemistically called "breakfast rations."

He looked down at me, his mouth showing the hint of a wry smile. "I might have known you'd be the one to get in first with the question."

"Is that a compliment?"

"It's an innocent remark." Turning to the others,

he said, "Listen up, people. We're going to be one short. Tom won't be coming with us."

There was a murmur of comment. Lipless Vince, as I had mentally labeled him, was standing near me, arms folded. "Tom failed the search, did he?" I asked him.

He didn't look at me. "Yes." Vince was clearly a man of few words.

"So what did you catch Tom with?"

Vince turned his head slowly, as if, I thought, a small electric motor had kicked in. The light from the plane's open cabin door fell across his face, but he didn't blink. His black eyes focused on my face, he said, "You're Dana."

"I am. And you're Vince." My pleasant smile was wasted on his stony expression.

Joyce had dark eyes too, but at times there was intelligence and humor in them. Vince's dead stare was quite machinelike. I entertained myself by imagining that Vince was actually an android, and that if I knew the right place to press on the side of his skull, I could unfasten his face, swing it open like a door, and look into the blinking circuits inside his head.

Vince must have detected amusement on my face, because he snarled, "You girls are all the bloody same. Making a joke of everything. Never take anything seriouslike."

Vince's voice lacked the resonance I'd expect with his chunky, powerful body. I fancied it was a bit tinny, as though artificially created.

"Tom was hiding a miniature recorder and a mini-camera," said a deep voice behind us — a voice that

61

would have suited Vince infinitely better than his own. I turned around to see the speaker.

It was Rob of the putty nose and pointed chin. He went on, "Tom was quite aware that no spy devices were allowed, but he told me he'd take the chance."

I didn't respond to this, but Rob acted as though I had asked a question. "You ask why? Why gamble? Tom said he wanted insurance. He believed on having a card or two up his sleeve."

This got a contemptuous grunt from Vince. "When I was finished with Tom," Vince said, "the bastard was lucky to *have* an arm to put in his bloody sleeve." This thought seemed to please him, as he showed a row of small, even teeth in a rapid smile, which bloomed then faded so quickly I felt I almost could have imagined it.

Rob, although about the same height as Vince, had a much lighter, sloping-shouldered build. However, he didn't allow this physical reality to intimidate him. "Typical," he jeered. "Brutes like you act, you don't think."

Apparently Vince didn't consider this an insult, as he said, unmoved, "I follow orders."

"Okay, everyone on board," Brit announced. She was wearing a camouflage suit, cut flatteringly to show her excellent figure. Fergus, clutching his brown-paper breakfast bag, rushed forward to be first on the aircraft, and I heard him say to Brit, "Can I sit with you?"

"I've been tossed aside," I said to Rob. "Flying up from Sydney, Fergus wanted to sit with *me*."

"Well, *I'd* like your company," he said, rather gallantly.

As I was intending to be at least second-best

friends with everyone at Camp E, the flight was an opportunity to get to know the three new people a little better. I'd start with Rob and then see if I could move on to Patsy. As for Vince, I doubted if a mere woman would ever get even to tenth-best friend with him, but I was willing to put in the effort later, when I was a little more on the ball.

The plane had a narrow center aisle with five rows of two seats each side. Rob and I sat near the back, and I waved him to the position next to the window so I could sit on the aisle. This was not politeness on my part, but an automatic survival technique, as I had seen studies showing that window-seat passengers on jets had slightly worse odds of getting out of a crash alive. Although I had no idea if the theory applied to little toy aircraft like this one, I figured it couldn't hurt to follow it.

There was much rustling as people examined their breakfast bags. I heard no cries of appreciation, and as I didn't feel the slightest hungry, I didn't bother opening mine.

"Not eating?" I said to Rob, who had tucked his bag under his seat.

He gave me a conspiratorial grin. "Can I confess something to you?"

"Possibly, but you don't know me. I could be a total blabbermouth."

"I'll take that chance. The fact is, I've already eaten breakfast. From a fast-food place called Speedy Ann's. And it was pretty good, too — bacon, eggs, coffee, the works."

"How come you're so favored? *I* wasn't offered a fast-food breakfast."

"Neither was I. Sneaked down to the office where

there's a pay phone and called a cab, asked him where the nearest place was, and I paid him to collect a meal and bring it back to me. Gave him a humongous tip, too."

I looked at Rob with undisguised admiration. "You're quite an operator!"

"Thanks."

There was no flight attendant to check to see if we were all wearing our seat belts, but the pilot, whose cockpit wasn't walled off from the passengers, twisted around in his seat to tell us all to buckle up, and shortly after that the little plane leapt up into the dark air and began to drone its way west.

I glanced over at Rob, who had his nose pressed against the glass trying to see out. Dawn was breaking behind us, and the back edge of the wing was touched with red light. I ran Rob through my mental checklist. Nationality: Australian. Age: early thirties. Build: weedy. Hair: receding, dark brown. Eyes: dark, probably brown. Nose: unforgettable.

That was the trouble with having a feature so unusual that people's eyes were automatically drawn to it. An Identi-Kit might not get his long ears, the faint white scar on his forehead, his pointed chin — but any witness would certainly remember Rob's nose.

It wasn't bulbous or red or pockmarked. It was *shapeless*. As soon as I saw it I called it a putty nose, but I might just as well have characterized it as melted wax or modeling clay.

If it had been my nose, I'd have hit it with plastic surgery in a minute, but maybe Rob wasn't worried about his looks. Perhaps, I thought, he was proud of it because it was a family nose, passed by dominant genes from generation to generation.

Rob broke into my fanciful thoughts by turning from the window and saying, "Do you know where we're going?"

"Some place called Kununurra."

"No, I mean the region, the Kimberleys."

I shook my head. "Not really."

In theory I knew the area well. To commit it to memory, I had started by visualizing the Kimberley region as being roughly a square containing over four hundred thousand square kilometers of rugged landscape. The north and west sides were made up of serrated coastline, where over eons the ocean had sculpted a myriad of gulfs and inlets. Many of these waterways were untamed and isolated, and populated by seabirds and fearsome saltwater crocodiles.

The south side of the square was marked by the Great Northern Highway, with the city of Broome, famous in history for pearl diving, in the bottom left-hand corner. Below this southern border of the Kimberleys stretched the forbidding wastes of the Great Sandy Desert.

Our plane was approaching the eastern side of the square. This, like the southern side, was marked by the Great Northern Highway, which looped north at tiny Halls Creek. Near the top right-hand corner of the imaginary square was the settlement of Wyndham, and to the south of it our destination, Kununurra.

Our aircraft droned on, its engines giving a comforting, muted roar. The sky lightened to day. Down the front of the cabin, Fergus was talking nonstop to

Brit, and snatches of his words drifted back to us. "Did I tell you about . . ."

Konrad, stooping in the confined space, came around to give out drinks — a choice of bottled water, orange juice, or ginger ale.

"No Coke? I need a caffeine fix."

Konrad's wide mouth turned up in a genuine smile. "Sorry, Dana, we don't serve addicts here."

With bad grace I took a carton of orange juice. From my seated vantage point I was practically looking up Konrad's nostrils, so I took the opportunity to compare his broken nose to Rob's amorphous one, deciding that Konrad's was preferable, as its crooked shape, although not pretty, at least hinted at a devil-may-care attitude.

Deciding that my fixation on external breathing organs was getting out of hand, I concentrated on chatting with Rob about inconsequential things. Neither of us said anything significant, and we both avoided anything personal in our conversation.

Two hours into the flight, Brit came up the aisle wearing her usual luminous smile. "Now everybody, I'm asking you to change seats. We're all going to be working together at Camp E, and getting to know every member of the group will help us all to achieve so much more."

"This switching seats idea is just so you can rid of Fergus, isn't it?" I said to Brit when she drew level to me.

She reddened slightly, but said firmly, "Of course not, Dana. This is standard management practice."

"It is? Well, I'm all for it, then."

I grabbed my brown bag, and with a little maneuvering I managed to plunk myself next to Patsy. "Hi, I'm Dana."

"Yes, I heard your name last night. And, if you'd been listening, you'd know my name is Patsy."

Close up, she was older than I'd thought, perhaps early fifties. Her hair was graying, and there was a network of fine lines on her face. She wasn't fat, but rather well-covered, with a substantial bust and dimpled elbows. Last night I'd taken her to be hearty and genial, but now her incisive tone made me suspect I would have to amend that first impression.

"Visited the Kimberleys before?" she asked, carefully peeling a fat banana she'd taken from her capacious, daisy-printed bag. Clearly Patsy didn't rely on the provisioning of others for sustenance.

"No, never," I said, looking dolefully into my breakfast bag. It contained a muesli bar, a small bag of dried apricots, an oatmeal-and-raisin slice tightly enclosed in plastic wrap, and a rather shriveled apple. Where to start?

"My husband, Des, and I did a tour of the Kimberley area three years ago. That was before the cancer, of course. It was enjoyable, but we never really went off the beaten track, just stuck with the tried and true. Know what I mean?"

She waved the banana around for emphasis, and for some reason I was irresistibly reminded of a large yellow penis.

"I reckon this time," she went on, "I'll be seeing the *real* Kimberleys, up close and personal, like they say."

Patsy circumcised the banana with one swift bite, then chewed thoughtfully. "Des and I were here in the

Dry. It's still the Wet now, you know, so conditions won't be ideal."

My briefings had taught me there were really only two seasons in the Kimberleys, the Wet and the Dry. The Wet was well named. Running from October through to the beginning of April, waterfalls gushed, rivers rose, dirt roads became muddy traps. The Dry, running from April to September, was when, had I the choice, I would have visited the Kimberleys. Warm to hot days, crisp, cool nights, and no rain.

"What's your specialty?" asked Patsy. She popped the last of the banana into her mouth and waited, her jaws moving, for my answer.

Presuming that she meant where my interest lay as far as radical action was concerned, I said, "Broad spectrum, actually."

She swallowed, sealed the banana peel into a plastic container, then dived into her bag again, retrieving a large bag of trail mix. "Really? I've always thought it better to concentrate on one field."

"And what is your field?"

Her unremarkable features were contorted by an expression of deep loathing. "So-called scientific advances," she ground out. "Stem cells, cloning, playing God with genes. The whole Frankenstein thing. It's got to be stopped, by any means available."

She suddenly jabbed me with her forefinger. "What do you think of medical experimentation, eh? Ethics are down the gurgler. You agree?"

"Oh, absolutely."

Patsy settled back in her seat. "Tried to persuade me to let them use something new and experimental on Des to treat his cancer. Riddled with it, he was. I said to the doctors: No beating around the bush, now.

Is this radical Frankenstein stuff?" Her lip curled with scorn. "They couldn't give me a straight answer, so I said, No way do you get near Des. No way is he going to be your guinea pig."

"What did Des think?"

Patsy frowned. "Des think? He agreed with me, naturally." She ripped open the trail mix, poured a generous portion into one hand, and threw it into her mouth. Indistinctly, she added, "Des died a few months later, but he had the satisfaction of knowing he wasn't a party to any radical, godless regimen."

"It must have been a comfort to him."

Patsy flicked a look at me, but my sympathetic face convinced her I wasn't having a go at her, so she nodded, saying, "It was. A great comfort to both of us."

She masticated another mouthful of trail mix, then said, "I got him. Professor Potter. The one who wanted to experiment on Des. That was the really satisfying thing."

"Got him?"

Patsy's face was suffused with pleasure. "Outside the Potter Institute for Cancer Research one rainy night in Melbourne a couple of weeks after Des died. I'd been watching, so I had his routine down pat. Waited with my engine running until he was in the middle of the road, hit the accelerator, and *wham!*"

She leaned over to her floral bag and this time came up with a silver thermos flask. Every caffeine-deprived cell in my body silently shrieked *It isn't fair!* as Patsy poured steaming coffee into the metal cup that formed the lid of the thermos, and took a sip. —"Ah!—" she said. "That really hits the spot."

To stop myself from too obviously yearning in the

direction of the coffee, I said, "So you killed this professor?"

"Not at all." Patsy smiled, reliving the memory. "Potter's a paraplegic now." Her face darkened as she added viciously, "I'd say he thinks his research on embryos will grow his spinal cord again. Fat chance!"

"You took a risk," I said.

"Not much of a risk. Had it planned down to the last detail. Didn't hit Potter square — that would have thrown him up into the windscreen — but more a glancing blow. Then I took off, went home, washed down the car to get rid of any blood, and took it down the street and ran it straight into a tree." She gave a snort of laughter. "Insurance paid for the whole lot. A real laugh, isn't it?"

"Quite a coup," I said, not feeling like laughing at all.

"But that's not the best thing," said Patsy. "When I finish this course I'm going back to Melbourne to blow up the whole bloody Potter Institute. Now that'll be a real coup, won't it?"

CHAPTER NINE

By the time we landed at Kununurra, the major
airport for the area, I had consumed everything in my
breakfast bag, plus heard more than I ever needed to
know about Fergus's early life and the influences that
had driven him to become an anarchist.

This had been an unavoidable trial, because when
Brit initiated the next seat change, accomplished with
great difficulty in the cramped space, I had found
myself having to take the only vacant place, which
happened to be next to Fergus.

I hadn't gone easily — looking around to find the

spare seat that Tom would have occupied, but Mokhtar had appropriated two seats to stretch out and sleep, so it was next to Fergus or the floor. By the time Fergus had got to the minutiae of his stint in the U.S. Army and the philosophical insights it had given him, I had decided the floor would have been a better bet. Hell, crammed into a storage locker with my chin on my knees seemed attractive.

There was one positive point however: I discovered why Fergus's face had seemed so familiar the first time I'd seen him. "I had a television career in L.A.," he confided.

"Really?"

"Made a commercial, an ad for tourism in the States. It was shown overseas, so you might have seen it. I played the raw, masculine spirit of the West."

"I recall the commercial," I said, delighting Fergus. I didn't add that I remembered it because it was so embarrassingly bad that in Australia it had been the subject of much spoofing in comedy shows.

"I haven't seen you in anything else," I said.

Fergus looked glum. "I was typecast," he said. "They looked at me, they saw the spirit of the West. Happens to the best of us. My career was over before it really began."

It was pouring with rain when the plane touched down, and the blast of hot, wet air that greeted us was a warning of what we were going to face in the bush.

The motel we were taken to was quite a step up from the one in Darwin. Located on a charming street with palm trees dotted down the median strip, the motel consisted of a series of low buildings, each with a red metal roof, generous verandas, and a wide-bladed ceiling fan in every room.

I would have liked to explore, if only to get over the cramped, claustrophobic feeling that came from being cooped up in a little plane, but we were not, however, free to roam. Rooms were shared — I was in with Patsy — and we were advised that we would be eating together at the motel's dining room, no exceptions allowed.

Although sure that ASIO knew exactly where I was, as all they needed was a glance at the flight plan of the aircraft to establish our group's destination, I still needed to call Livia and give her the information I'd already gleaned about Edification personnel, plus details of Patsy and Fergus.

We'd been expressly told not to carry mobile phones, and if anyone had disobeyed this instruction, I was sure the cell phone would have been confiscated in Darwin. That left the phone in the room. As a test run, and hoping later I could get rid of Patsy some way, I picked up the receiver when Patsy disappeared into the bathroom. I couldn't automatically get an outside line when I pressed the appropriate numbers, so I rang through to the front office to find out why. I was informed that TrekTrak had requested that phone services not be provided to tour participants' rooms.

Replacing the receiver, I thought that probably it was a good thing I couldn't dial out. Edification could easily check that I had called someone. True, even if they knew the number I would have dialed, it'd have been disconnected after my first contact, but nevertheless it could look suspicious, and that was something I wanted to avoid at all costs.

"Who were you trying to call?" asked Patsy, coming out of the bathroom.

"Pizza delivery. I'm starving to death here, but it's no go — Edification's blocked the lines so we can't call out."

Patsy gave an unsympathetic grunt. "Be prepared, like me. I never go anywhere without my own store of food and drink."

By dinner I was truly ravenous. The dining room was furnished with cane and glass, and the ubiquitous ceiling fans turned slowly overhead. We were seated four to a table, and I found myself with Mokhtar, Brit, and a man I had never seen before.

There could hardly have been a greater contrast between Mokhtar and this stranger. Where Mokhtar was slight, this guy was sturdy. Mokhtar was olive skinned, fine-featured, and had dark hair and eyes; this man had hair that was almost white and fair skin, red and flaking on his nose and cheeks. His features were coarse, as though he missed out on the final refining touches. I noticed that the backs of his hands were spotted and peeling.

Brit flashed her pearly, capped teeth. "Dana, Mokhtar, this is Gary. Gary — Dana, Mokhtar."

We all murmured appropriately, then Brit said, "Gary and Aaron are joining us here for the sixteen-hour drive to our destination."

I focused on the time period, thinking with a groan of sixteen hours jolting around in a four-wheel drive. Mokhtar's attention was on something else altogether. "Aaron is a Jewish name. Is this man a Jew?"

Taken aback, Brit said, "I don't know. Does it matter?"

"It does."

In a nasal drawl, Gary observed, "Anti-Semitic, are you, mate? Well, you're out of luck. Aaron's Jewish."

Mokhtar straightened his shoulders, glaring at Gary with burning intensity. "I cannot ride in a vehicle with this person."

"No worries. We've got three Land Cruisers."

As Mokhtar's upright stance relaxed a little, I put in my contribution. "Heavens, Mokhtar, half of us could be Jewish, and you'd never know."

His finely arched eyebrows plunged into a deep frown. He turned to Gary, who put up his hand in a stop-right-there gesture. "No, mate, you don't get any more concessions. You can switch to whatever vehicle you want, but that's it. If you don't like Jews, then too bad. You can bail right now if it's going to be a problem."

Mokhtar reached for a menu, flipped it open, and began to study its contents. Gary leaned over and took it from him. "Mate, I need to know if this is a problem you can't handle."

Brit, her face hard, was watching both of them with close attention. At times like this I saw the steel under the glossy surface.

"Well?" said Gary.

"I can handle it."

"Good," said Gary, handing the menu back to Mokhtar. "Now that's settled, let's order."

I slept very well, even though Patsy turned out to be a snorer who woke me at least twice with deafening snorting sounds. As I drifted back to sleep, I reflected how ironic it would be if Patsy were to die of severe sleep apnea before she had the opportunity to blow up the Potter Cancer Institute.

She was still alive at sunrise, which was rise-and-shine time. Patsy, it turned out, was one of those people unable to shine before midmorning, and all I heard from her were a few sullen grunts when I kindly inquired whether she felt rested after her night's sleep.

Driven by a devilish impulse I couldn't resist, I said to her, "You know, I'd get that sleep apnea looked at, Patsy. You're depriving your brain cells of oxygen, and that can't be good for them."

"What?"

"It's very common, especially if you lie on your back to sleep, like you do."

"I don't have it."

"Yes you do, but you wouldn't know, because you're asleep at the time."

Patsy slammed the bathroom door behind her, which I interpreted as indicating that the subject was closed.

The three Toyota Land Cruisers had diesel engines, and their mud-splattered bodies showed they'd ploughed their way through difficult conditions. Brit, ever efficient, directed each of us to the 4WD in which we were to travel for the first leg of the journey. I was in the first one with Vince and Rob, Aaron driving; Fergus and Patsy were in the second Toyota and had Gary as their driver; Brit and Mokhtar were in the third, with Joyce at the wheel.

"This model's the one to have around here," said Aaron, who turned out to be a tanned, no-nonsense sort of guy with heavy-lidded eyes, a slow smile, and a cigarette drooping from his bottom lip.

He continued in his leisurely cadence. "Think you'll find it's the most popular four-wheeler in the Outback." He delivered an affectionate slap to the side of our 4WD. "Take you to hell and back."

Turning his face up to the steel gray sky, which was threatening a downpour at any moment, he said, "Hope you lot are good at handling a shovel. Looks like we could be digging out any number of times."

"Are you serious?" said Rob, obviously appalled at the idea of wading around in a quagmire.

Aaron chuckled. "Dead serious," he said. "You haven't lived until you've got yourself knee deep in mud with your shoulder against the Toyota, trying to heave it out of the muck."

I was speedy enough to snaffle the front seat beside Aaron, a fact that seemed to annoy Vince no end. "You'd be better in the back," he said, opening the door I'd just closed, apparently to encourage me to hop out. "Besides, that's my seat."

Swinging himself behind the wheel, Aaron said, "First in, first served, Vince old mate. You can rough it in the back. It'll be good for you." To me he said, "You stay there Dana. Don't let him intimidate you."

Vince's face was hard as stone. "Are you going to move?"

"No."

He slammed my passenger door with much more force than necessary, and climbed into the seat behind me. Rob, who was already belted in, observed that it was probably better for traction to have the weight in the back, and that Vince looked mighty heavy to him. Aaron and I grinned. I couldn't see Vince's face, but I doubted he was smiling with us.

Our Toyota leading, the three-vehicle convoy splashed out of the motel parking area and set off for the Gibb River Road. Aaron was quite happy to explain where we were going, and I traced our route on my mental map.

The unpaved Gibb River Road ran diagonally across the region, eventually ending at Derby on King Sound. We would be traveling roughly the first third of it, then turning at the junction of the Kalumburu Road, which led north to the settlement of Kalumburu way up on the coastline. We wouldn't be going that far: about a hundred and seventy kilometers north of the Gibb River Road junction we would turn west onto the Mitchell Plateau Track.

At last I knew approximately where Camp E was located. I squeezed my eyes shut to visualize the area. The Mitchell River National Park was situated in some of the most remote and inaccessible country in Australia. The Mitchell Plateau was edged with sandstone gorges, cut by rivers and streams. There was a riot of wildlife, including, I recalled, death adder and taipan snakes.

"Will we get there tonight?" asked Rob. "Brit said sixteen hours traveling time."

"Not bloody likely!" Aaron was mightily amused. "Brit was a bit optimistic, there. It'll take us two days, maybe more if the road's washed out."

As it happened, Brit wasn't that far off as far as total traveling time was concerned, although parts of the Gibb River Road were in bad condition. The first night we stayed overnight at a fairly primitive road-house that in better days had built a set of little cottages for rent. Now they were dilapidated and leaking, but after the jolting ride we'd had all day, they were comfort itself.

The next day we hit the really rough roads, and as I was now in the backseat, Vince having seized the prized front position, I was jolted around even more than before. To add to our misery, it began to rain hard. Amazingly, not one of the Toyotas got stuck, which was a credit both to the vehicles and the drivers, and we made reasonable time.

Turning onto the Mitchell Plateau Track, however, led us to truly atrocious conditions. The road was washed away in parts, and on several occasions all of us had to pile out and help get one or other of the vehicles out of a mud trap. The rain had slacked off as we left the track itself and struck out into what seemed virgin bushland, although it was clear that Aaron knew exactly where he was going.

Wet, muddy, and exhausted, we finally arrived at Camp E, which consisted of camouflage tents so artfully hidden that we were in the middle of the camp before we realized it was there. Our little convoy pulled up outside the largest tent, the roar of the diesel engines was stilled, and blessed silence descended.

As, with various degrees of effort, we clambered out of the vehicles, a woman wearing shorts and a khaki T-shirt came out of the tent to greet us. I glanced at her, then looked again. She was sensational — long-legged, with a mane of chestnut hair, an exotic, high-cheeked face, and a blinding smile.

"Everyone," said Brit, conscientious to the end, but when smeared with mud and sweat not quite her usual ebullient self, "meet Siobhan."

Fergus, fatigued though he might be, was plainly smitten. "What's your name again?"

"Siobhan."

"She-born? Sher-vorn? Have I got it right?"

"Somewhere between the two."

Fergus frowned. "What kind of name is that?"

"Irish."

He nodded wisely. "Ah, I see," he said, although her smile indicated she didn't think he saw at all.

CHAPTER TEN

We took turns in the bush shower, an ingenious contraption consisting of a canvas cubicle with open wooden slats for a floor and a container of water overhead. Pull the cord, and a spray descended on you — release it, and the flow stopped. The idea was to get wet, then shut off the water and lather up, before rinsing off. At least there was no shortage of water. The rain had let up for the moment, but there was a growl of thunder overhead, and the clouds were so low I felt I could reach up through the top of the shower cubicle and touch them.

There were two bush showers, side by side, and next to me I could hear a male singing "Oklahoma" off key, but with enthusiasm. Just as the wind came sweeping down the plains for the fourth time I wound a mercifully large towel around me, shoved my feet into my muddy boots, grabbed my things, and skittered out the canvas flap and down the row of tents until I could dive into mine.

Each of us had our own little gray-green tent — with the emphasis on *little*. Brit had assured us that they were top of the line, with a floor that was integral to the structure so that insects and other creatures could not enter, and mesh panels to allow a free flow of air. Once my luggage was inside there was just enough room for the camp bed, a lantern, a red plastic washing bowl, an enamel mug, and a clear plastic water bottle complete with carrying strap. Standing upright was an impossibility, so I had to get dressed by assuming various contorted positions.

I spread my towel over my suitcase to dry, sprayed myself with insect repellent, and followed instructions to close the entry flap carefully. As Brit had said with a grimace, "Otherwise, there'll be awful creepy-crawlies waiting for you."

Camp E was larger than I had at first thought, and well concealed. The location was near a long out-cropping of rock, and adjacent to a small stream. Tents were pitched under the shelter of large trees, so from the air the camp would be close to invisible.

Extreme hunger impelled me toward the central meeting place, a large marquee-style tent with side walls that could be rolled up to let in the breeze. It was getting dark, and the walls were all down, probably to avoid having the lights shine out like a beacon that could attract both insects and any other people who might be in the wilderness area.

Inside there were trestle tables and benches. Lighting was provided by pressure lamps hung from each corner, and additional lamps sitting on the tables. The most welcome sight was at one end of the area — trestles bearing two silver urns, one labeled COFFEE and the other HOT WATER, and a jumbo-size container from which rose enticing steam. A lightly built young woman with a tight little face and neat movements was dishing out a delicious-smelling stew, and I hastily stepped up behind Mokhtar to join the growing queue.

I looked around for Siobhan, wondering if she would strike me as equally stunning at second viewing. I spotted her over to one side talking to Joyce, and was gratified to find she was still a total knockout, although she was far from conventionally beautiful. Of course, it could have been the faintly golden, flattering light thrown by the lamps that made her seem so attractive. I rather hoped it enhanced me, too.

Keep your mind on your job, I chided myself. But then, my job entailed getting as much information as possible. It was clearly my duty to cultivate relationships.

Although too far away to hear anything of what they were saying, I observed their conversation with interest. Being shorter, Joyce looked up at Siobhan, but she didn't seem to be at a disadvantage. From their faces I judged the subject at hand was something serious, so I was disconcerted when they both looked in my direction. The familiar prickle of disquiet tickled my spine. Was I the topic under discussion? And if I was, why?

Distracted, I bumped into Mokhtar, who was ahead

of me in the line. Quick as a cat he swung around, a muffled curse, not in English, on his lips. His eyes narrowed. "Oh, it's you."

"Sorry, didn't mean to run into you."

Up this close, Mokhtar's smooth skin was perfection, and his dark eyes and hair made a wonderful contrast. He was, at least physically, compellingly handsome.

"I don't like to be touched," he said very softly, his face close to mine. "It would be wise for you to remember that."

"It'll be difficult," I said, "but I'll try to keep my hands off you."

"Move it along," someone hungry yelled, breaking up our staring contest.

A few minutes later, plate of stew in one hand and a chunk of crusty bread in the other, I looked around for a seat. Vince was sitting all alone at the table nearest to me, and when he saw me hesitating, his slash of a mouth turned down at the corners. "This table's reserved," he announced. "You'll have to go somewhere else."

I favored him with a sunny smile. "Don't tell me you're still holding a grudge because I sat in the front seat yesterday?"

I imagined circuits behind his opaque eyes lighting up with activity as Vince's expression abruptly changed from disagreeable to downright nasty. "You're full of it!" he spat out.

Looking over his head, I spied an empty table at the other end of the tent. "I'd love to continue our talk," I said with polite regret, "but I'm afraid I must go."

Making my way to the unoccupied bench, I mused

on the unfortunate fact that although I saw my job as getting on with everyone, two people — Mokhtar and Vince — regarded me with aversion. I reassured myself that this might be advantageous, as it would be suspicious if I were too Pollyannaish.

I sat down with anticipation, breathing in the steam that rose from my stew. "It's on its way, stomach," I murmured, breaking off a chunk of bread.

"Dana!" The plate Fergus held looked small in his large hand. He raised his sandy eyebrows hopefully. "May I join you?"

"Of course," I said, neutral in the enthusiasm department, but certainly not unwelcoming. My attention was on my food, so Fergus could burble on as much as he liked. It wouldn't bother me.

"I've been talking to Siobhan," he said, settling himself down opposite me. "Delightful woman." He appeared to have settled for a pronunciation close to *Shay-vorn* for her Gaelic name.

I dunked my bit of bread in my stew, then popped it into my mouth. Heaven!

"She's English, just like you."

Heaven receded a little. Could Siobhan possibly have known Dana Wright?

"I'm not English, I'm Australian," I said in my clipped, modified accent.

"You sound English to me."

"Surely I mentioned to you," I said, knowing I hadn't, "that I've been living in Britain for years?"

I made haste to take another mouthful before Fergus could say anything else to ruin this surprisingly sublime dining experience.

Fergus cocked his head. "That makes your brother an Aussie too."

"That's right." I was offhand. This wasn't a topic I wanted to discuss. In Sydney Fergus had shown entirely too much interest in my "insane brother" as he kept calling Norbert, and had been obviously disappointed when I proved unwilling to fill in all the gruesome details about Norbert's crime.

As my instructor had pointed out countless times, "If you don't talk about it, you can't be tripped up by something you've said." Just this once I was taking his advice, and trying to keep off anything to do with Dana's life in Britain.

Still, I was tempted to ask if Fergus had any recent information. I'd tried to scan television news programs at the Kununurra motel, but Patsy had her favorite shows to watch, and news definitely wasn't one of them. When I had managed to wrest the control from her, all I'd got that night were bits and pieces of various other items, but nothing at all about the manhunt. Since then there hadn't been an opportunity to listen to radio or watch television.

Fergus tried his stew. "Not bad." In short order he polished off the whole plateful. Now that his mouth was unoccupied, he took the opportunity to smile winningly at me. "You're cool, I'll say that much for you."

"I am?"

"You must have heard your brother's supposed to be heading this way. If he talks like you, he'll stick out like a sore thumb."

Suddenly my food didn't taste quite so good. "This way? To the Kimberleys?"

Fergus looked puzzled. "No, not here — heading to Australia, probably Sydney. I picked it up on a CNN news flash the night before last. Weren't you watching?"

Repressing an impulse to snarl at him that obviously I hadn't been watching CNN, I said mildly, "If I had seen the newscast, then I'd know all about it now, wouldn't I? And I don't."

"Well, yeah, you would."

"Are you going to tell me what's happening?"

"Sure. The cops in France picked up the woman your brother was on the run with. Belle? Nell? Something like that."

"Nellie. Nellie Banks."

Fergus nodded, satisfied. "Yes, that's it, Nellie. Seems he cleaned her out cashwise, then dumped her. She's boo-hooing all the way to the bank, of course, selling her story to the London papers, but first she wants to get back at him, so she spills everything she knows to the cops."

"What *does* she know about Norbert's plans?" I asked, hoping to speed up his delivery of the story.

"Norbert! That's the name I've been trying to remember. You know when it's on the tip of your tongue . . ."

Fergus apparently would never get to the point. Perhaps if I grabbed him by the collar and shook him until his teeth rattled . . .

I said in an astringent tone, "I really would appreciate it, Fergus, if you would tell me why anyone believes that my brother would come to Australia."

"This Nellie woman said that Norbert's on a mission."

I'd seen the results of Norbert on one of those before. Details of the crime-scene photographs flashed across my mind: a skull split open, an arm almost severed, deep defense wounds on his mother's hands — and everywhere blood, blood, blood.

Perhaps my face showed some of my thoughts, because suddenly a look of deep concern flooded Fergus's face. "You know, when I think of it, I should have found you and made sure you knew what was happening." He shook his head, apparently regretting his failure. "I'd guess the authorities are looking for you right now, to warn you."

I was sure I knew the answer, but still said, "Warn me about what, specifically?"

"This Nellie woman told the cops that your brother had fixed himself up with a fake passport, and when he found out from one of your friends in London that you'd flown to Sydney, he told her he had to go after you. Said it was essential to finish what he'd started, and that it was his mission to kill you."

Fergus paused, then said, almost apologetically, "Apparently his actual words were, 'I'm going to chop her into little pieces.' "

"Norbert was always a nasty little boy," I said with a bit of a grin. Fergus didn't smile.

CHAPTER ELEVEN

"Your attention please, people!" Konrad's voice rose above the hubbub of conversation. "I know you've had a long day, but Brit has a few things to say to you, and then I'll be going through some necessary information to help everything run smoothly."

He'd changed into a short-sleeved shirt, and I was interested to see that his snake tattoo, as I suspected, did spiral up his arm, ending with the tail curled around his biceps.

Brit, glossy hair restored to its shampoo-commercial best, bounded up to join Konrad, her smile slickly professional. "Before I start, I'd like to congratulate Corrina for her excellent catering tonight." She indicated the young woman who'd been serving out the stew. "Corrina and Aaron are responsible for all meals, and for the day-to-day running of Camp E. If you have any problems in this area, please see one of them."

"Great tucker," said a man I hadn't met. He was a nothing sort of person, with a face that you see once and instantly forget.

"That reminds me," said Brit, "that we haven't all met. Wade, Cliff, and Evonne came up from Broome a few days ago and have really settled into the camp routine. That's Wade, who just spoke." Wade made a mock bow. "Cliff, where are you?"

"Here." A young man, who looked no more than eighteen, stood up, blushing. He had ginger hair, freckles, and a shy smile.

Brit craned her neck. "And Evonne?"

A square woman with a short, thick neck partly hidden by her long, curly hair raised her hand. "I'm here."

Brit nodded approvingly. "Well, people, you can all get to know each other when we break for coffee."

I was delighted to hear of a coffee break, as extra caffeine might help me reestablish my equilibrium, which had been shaken by the fact that Norbert was on his way to Australia. I couldn't imagine how the British security services could have missed this friend who seemed to have known about Dana's plans. And if this mysterious friend knew that, perhaps he or she also had information on Edification.

I couldn't ignore what Fergus had told me. The real Dana would be, to say the least, worried by the news, and would certainly want to raise the subject with Konrad or one of the others.

My attention came back to Brit, who had been delivering a motivational spiel, and was now winding up to a climax.

". . . and so, everyone, we will all be pulling together to increase our knowledge, our skills. Your nationalities, your politics, your beliefs — all are irrelevant here. What is important is that we respect each other as people."

She paused, possibly expecting applause — none materialized — then yielded the floor to Konrad. He was much more pragmatic and succinct. He detailed camp rules, all commonsense items, and outlined briefly the regimen that would be followed every day except the seventh rest day, which could be spent any way we chose, as long as we stayed within the environs of the camp. He cautioned us to be careful of the terrain, which was harsh and unforgiving.

Konrad repeated some key points. It was essential that our presence in the Mitchell Plateau area not be suspected, so no lights were to show at night, as they could be seen for some distance. If any aircraft, particularly helicopters, were in the area we were to stay under cover. Lastly, in the unlikely event that any of us were to run into someone outside the camp, we were to make sure that it was clear that we were here on an ecotour with TrekTrak.

When everyone broke for coffee I made my way toward the front where Konrad was talking with Siobhan and Gary. Before I got there I was waylaid by the woman with the thick neck. "G'day, I'm Evonne. I seen you before."

My stomach plummeted. Where before? When I

was Denise? I couldn't believe I'd forget this woman if I'd met her previously. She was short, solid, and formidable. The only soft thing about her was her hair, which fell in incongruous long ringlets to her heavy shoulders.

"You've seen me before?" I said, bouncing on my mental toes so I'd be ready to fabricate a story if I had to cover myself.

"Yeah. When you arrived at E this arvo. Cripes, you were a mess, the whole lot of you. Mud from head to foot. I had to laugh."

I gave her a weak smile as relief swept over me. No kidding, I was going to have to get a grip. This tendency to think the worst was shredding my nerves.

"You using your own name?" She had the manner of one who always expected fast answers to any question she asked.

"Yes — it's Dana."

Evonne wrinkled her nose. "Dana, eh? Don't like it much."

"It suits me."

"Yeah," said Evonne, looking me over. "S'pose it does." She twirled a ringlet around a thick forefinger. "Me, I unloaded my moniker in a flash. Bloody parents, the things they do to you."

I made an indeterminate noise that could have been agreement. How was I going to get away from this blasted woman?

"Would you believe," Evonne said, "they landed me with Gladys? Gladys! Used to call me 'Our Glad,' till I could've barfed."

"It must have been difficult for you."

"Difficult? Reckon you can guess what the bastards at school did with a name like Gladys. I was fed up,

92

so I got a book of baby names and picked Evonne. More like me, as a person, I mean, don't you think?"

"Oh, definitely."

"I spell it with an *E*, not a *Y*. Seems neater."

I was contemplating outright rudeness when I was rescued by Joyce. "Dana, can I speak with you for a moment?" She'd taken her hair out of its usual ponytail, and it framed with lank strands her thin, intense face.

"Excuse me," I said to Evonne, who was obviously disappointed to lose a promising audience. As I turned to go, inspiration struck. "Have you met Fergus?" I said to her, pointing him out. "He's very interested in names."

As we watched Evonne plow her way toward Fergus, Joyce, laughing, said, "You're very wicked, you know that, don't you?"

"Purely self-defense."

"Can I get you a coffee?" Joyce was positively effusive. "And a coconut slice? They're very good."

I gestured in the direction of Konrad, Siobhan, and Gary, who were still deep in conversation. "Actually, I did want to speak with Konrad."

Joyce's pleasant expression disappeared. "Then I won't hold you up."

I was aware of her dark stare as I threaded my way between the tables. As I joined the three of them I looked sideways at Siobhan, wondering if there was the slightest possibility that she could have met Dana Wright in England. If she had, I'd know soon enough.

"I'm sorry to interrupt," I said, "but I may have a bit of a problem."

"About your brother?" said Konrad.

I must have looked as astonished as I felt, because

he gave me an understanding smile. "We know he's threatened to find you. In fact, we've been discussing it."

"How did you know?"

Gary, his fair skin even ruddier than usual in the soft lighting, said to me, "Patsy and I have just spent two days cooped up in the Toyota with Fergus. Fair dinkum, that bloke has verbal diarrhea — talked about himself nonstop. Anyway, along with his life history Fergus did mention a few other things, and one of them was the latest news about your brother intending to follow you to Australia."

Gary paused, then added with a sly smile, "I think Fergus is quite taken with you, Dana, you lucky girl."

Siobhan broke in to say, "We should discuss this in private. Dana, why don't you get a coffee and join us in the admin. tent?"

Her expression didn't show recognition, and she wasn't shouting that I was an imposter, so that was one worry out of the way.

The woman had an appealing English accent, not too plummy, but crisp. If a voice could have a color, hers would be a deep burgundy with silver highlights.

"Okay," I said, thinking it was a shame that Konrad and Gary would be there too. "See you in a mo."

Five minutes later, armed with a cardboard cup of coffee, I stepped out into blackness. Naturally there could be no betraying lights outside, but with only the faint glow coming through the walls of the meeting room, it was hard to make out anything at all.

My eyes gradually became accustomed to the darkness, and I realized the clouds had cleared and that the river of stars forming the Milky Way was providing illumination. Living so much in cities, I was always surprised anew to find how bright starlight could be when it wasn't drowned by the pervasive glow of civilization.

Even with the combined glow of millions of stars I still managed to trip over something and slosh hot coffee on my hand, but eventually I located the admin. tent and slipped through the flap.

"Come on over and get comfortable," said Konrad, beckoning me to the table where he, Siobhan, and Gary were sitting.

Getting comfortable probably wasn't in the cards. Instead of benches there were chairs, but they were those folding ones that have hard metal seats and tubular steel legs that pinch your fingers when you collapse the chair. Then I noticed that the tables in the tent were all trestles, which was not surprising, since they were easy to store and to transport.

Taking the spare chair, which was quite as uncomfortable as it looked, I made a space for my coffee in the mess of papers and folders that covered the tabletop. A quick glance around showed me more tables covered with papers, two three-drawer metal file cabinets, a metal cupboard, a large broadband radio, and a little battery-powered television set. Timetables and schedules were attached to the canvas walls.

In the far corner of the tent there was the bulky outline of equipment under a gray plastic cover. Seeing me looking in that direction, Konrad said, "A portable generator for emergency power, and a ham radio."

"No computer?" I asked.

"A couple of laptops and an inkjet printer, so we can produce additional material for the classes," said Siobhan, "although essentially all the course materials are here, ready to assemble." Her smile was rueful. "You wouldn't care to volunteer a little time, would you? There's a lot to collate before classes begin tomorrow afternoon."

The chance of spending a little time, quality or not, with Siobhan made the offer sound quite alluring. "Maybe," I said, "if you make it worth my while."

All business, Gary rapped impatiently on the table. I noticed that the backs of his hands, which I'd thought sunburnt and peeling when I'd first noticed them, actually seemed to have something closer to a skin disease.

"Let's get this clear, Dana," he said. "We're not actively trying to get information about the situation with your brother because we don't initiate any contact with the outside world. It's too risky. Anything can be traced anywhere these days, and intercepted messages have been the downfall of a lot of radical groups. Edification doesn't intend to be one of them, so we stay electronically silent, monitoring what we can with a satellite dish."

"What if there's an emergency?"

"We deal with it ourselves." A trick of shadows and light made Konrad's broken-nosed face look impossibly sinister. "In fact, during the last camp we had someone die from snakebite." He jerked his head toward the outside. "He's buried out there in the bush. Just one of the people who go missing, and never get found."

I shifted my feet, my wild imagination immediately populating the area under the table with a nest of serpents. "I'm not that keen on snakes," I said, then, as my glance caught Konrad's tattoo, I added quickly, "Decorative are okay."

He chuckled, tapping the back of his hand where the flat deadliness of the snake's head was depicted. "This is a taipan," he said. "Funnily enough, the kind of snake that killed him."

"Did you get the tattoo before, or after?"

Konrad looked at me, then threw back his head and laughed. "You're one of a kind, Dana."

"Norbert Cummins is the subject at hand," Gary snapped, immediately sobering Konrad, and reminding me I was supposed to be behaving like someone being stalked — in fact, I *was* someone being stalked.

Subdued, I said, "You're aware of my brother's history?"

"Of course." Gary was impatient.

I moved my shoulders uneasily. "He's totally unstable, and capable of anything, but he has a superficial, charming persona that fools most people."

"Like brother, like sister?" said Siobhan.

That hit me like a cold slap. Was she playing with me, knowing I wasn't Dana?

"Norbert's insane — I'm just a bit twisted," I said lightly. Then, seriously, "If he makes it to Australia, could he trace me here?"

"No way." Konrad was reassuringly definite. "We've closed the TrekTrak office in Sydney, and besides that, we've always made sure that everything was on a need-to-know basis. That means no one has enough information to point him in this direction."

"The problem," said Siobhan, "is that the media are beating the story to death, and any new angle will bring them down like a pack of wolves. We don't want anything that will draw attention to Edification's work, and all this notoriety means that journalists who aren't hacks will be digging, asking questions, trying to trace your whereabouts."

"Do you want me to quit the course?"

"Not at all," said Konrad, "but when it's finished, we'll have to get you out of here in a way that will throw anyone who gets close off the scent."

"Fly me out?"

"Have you picked up by sea, even though there's always a chance of bumping into boat people."

I knew exactly what Konrad was referring to — illegal immigrants. However, being Dana, who hadn't lived in Australia for many years, I had to appear puzzled by the reference. The long coast of Western Australia, with all its remote inlets and bays, made it a preferred target for people smugglers. A large proportion of the smugglers' vessels originated in Indonesia and sailed disguised as fishing boats. Coastwatch patrols had intercepted thousands of boat people, many from the Middle East, attempting to enter Australia in these remote areas. Sometimes they were abandoned by their transporters, and only luck and government vigilance saved hundreds of them from perishing in the wilderness.

While Gary gave me an explanation of what the term *boat people* meant, Konrad fiddled with a stapler. He interrupted to say, "Look, Dana doesn't need a potted history of immigration into this country. Let's concentrate on essentials here."

"And that would be?" Gary's expression showed his aggravation at the interruption.

"By now Fergus will have spread the story about

Dana's brother throughout the camp. We need to neutralize the issue. Say it's under control, that the integrity of Camp E hasn't been compromised, and that the schedule will run as expected."

I was still not sure who was in charge here. At first I would have said Konrad, but Gary and Siobhan both spoke as equals. A triumvirate perhaps?

"Who's in charge, here?" I said. When they all looked at me, I went on, "What I mean is, who do I go to if something . . . something important happens?"

Jeez, that sounded weak to me, but no one seemed surprised at my question. "Any of us," said Konrad. "We're all equals in Edification."

"Not Joyce," said Gary. A grin spread over his face. "Don't go to Joyce if you have a problem."

"No?"

"Joyce's got the hots for you. Every camp she picks out someone to have a bit of fun with, and this time it looks like you're it. I'd steer clear of her, if I were you."

CHAPTER TWELVE

Grabbing a pile of stapled sheets, Konrad said brusquely, "Better get back — everyone's tired and we still have to give them some stuff for tomorrow."

I let the others go first, all of us following the dancing red light of a modified pencil torch that Siobhan was shining on the ground ahead of us.

Gary's mocking comment about Joyce had thrown up a question to which I'd not found an answer. Dana Wright's sexuality was a puzzle. She'd certainly had close relationships with men while attending university, and she had also had several intense friendships with women, but once she had become fully involved in radical movements, Dana appeared to have become essentially sexless. In the last five years she'd dated no one, male or female.

Quite early in the piece Livia and I had discussed the issue as part of my preparation, and she had finally said, "Just see what happens. Play it as it goes."

"I think I'll continue Dana's lead and be sexless," I had declared. Livia, I recalled, had laughed immoderately.

It wasn't likely that Edification would have paid any attention to Dana Wright's close personal relationships — or lack of same. The point of interest would have been her political beliefs and actions, and in this area Dana had been beyond reproach.

Back in the main tent the hum of conversation was definitely muted by the fatigue of hard travel and the enervating effects of heat combined with high humidity, although Evonne seemed unaffected, having a dazed-looking Fergus firmly in her conversational grip.

"As I was saying, if my first hubby was trouble, my second was a bloody disaster. Cyrus, his name was, and that should have been warning enough —"

Frowning, Evonne broke off when Konrad began to speak. "Listen up, everyone, we need to cover just a few things before we wind up the evening."

Bearing Gary's warning in mind, I looked around for Joyce, and accidentally locked glances with her. Arms folded, she stared at me, haughty and withdrawn. I tried a friendly smile, but got no response.

What had I said or done to deserve this cool treatment? True, I'd turned down Joyce's offer of coffee and coconut slice, but that didn't seem grounds enough for the depth of this negative reaction. I got an inkling of the possible cause when Joyce's attention was taken by Siobhan, who was distributing the stapled sheets. The expression on Joyce's face was subtle, but if asked I would have described it as curdled dislike.

I raised a mental eyebrow. Was it, perhaps, that Joyce felt she had first dibs on me, and was concerned that Siobhan might muscle in? I was so tired that this frivolous thought made me giggle.

"Enjoying yourself?" said Rob, faintly smiling. "You must be, if you can raise a laugh."

He was so drawn that his skin was gray-yellow. Even his nose was a pale blob. "Are you all right?" I pushed him gently down onto the nearest bench. "Are you sick?"

"Migraine."

"That's awful. Have you got something to take?" My sympathy wasn't feigned. Although I'd never had one myself, I'd experienced them secondhand through my father, whose migraines had laid him low for days. I remembered how my brother, Martin, and I had crept around the darkened house, knowing that loud noise and light were unbearable to a migraine sufferer.

Rob, eyes screwed up in pain, said, "I've taken everything I can. A good night's sleep is what I need."

Putting my hand on his arm, I said, "Come on, I'll help you to your tent."

Rob put up his hand. "No way, Dana. Weaklings aren't encouraged here. I can last until the end."

We were the final ones to get the handouts. As Siobhan gave me my copy, she said, "If you would help out tomorrow, collating and stapling, I'd be very grateful."

I toyed with the idea of a flirtatious comment, but settled for, "Okay."

Over Siobhan's shoulder I caught sight of Brit. Her habitual smile absent, she was gazing in Siobhan's direction. Joyce's expression had indicated antagonism, but in Brit's case it wasn't dislike on her face, but total blankness. I'd become so accustomed to Brit's glib facial expressions that the absence of anything at all was surprisingly disturbing.

Konrad's voice rang out above the tired murmuring. "Everyone got a handout? Good, let's get on with it. The sheets you've just been given list the schedule of topics that will be covered in the coming weeks. Who will be doing what, and when, will be established before lunch tomorrow, so we will all meet here at eleven-thirty sharp."

"Regimented, like the bloody army," said the instantly forgettable Wade, his tone disparaging. I concentrated on committing his face to memory. He had nondescript hair and a face that was so ordinary that not one feature seemed individual. I checked his ears. Not a surprise to find nothing striking. Wade's height and build were, I was sure, the median for the adult male population of the country. He could have hired himself to the advertising industry as Mr. Average.

Ignoring Wade's comment, Konrad continued, "Tomorrow morning after breakfast you'll be familiarized with the facilities, the general area, and, most important, your individual responsibilities. Please check the last page . . ."

There was a rustle of paper as we obeyed. Konrad waited for a moment, then said, "This daily timetable sets out precise times for meals and classes. There is no give-and-take here: You are expected to be punctual. Excuses are not accepted."

Glancing through the scheduled classes, I thought that in a bizarre sort of way this was like a kids' special-interest camp, where those who shared enthusiasm for computers or swimming or botany or whatever could gather together. Our shared interest was rather more deadly, however, being the efficient commission of terrorist acts.

The syllabus covered a wide range: Simple Bomb Construction; Advanced Bomb Construction; Biological Weapons; Chemical Weapons; Arson; Ecoterrorism; Government Responses to Terrorism; Surveillance Techniques; Security in an Electronic World; Kidnapping; Disruption of Vital Services; Effective Propaganda; Interrogation Techniques; Strategies to Panic the Public; Cloaking Techniques; Tactics If Apprehended; Micro and Macro Management of Riots.

"One more thing," said Konrad. "Perhaps you've heard the rumor that one of you is associated with a sensational news story." Several people looked at me, then at Fergus, who had a pleased I-told-you-so expression on his face.

"The rumor is true," Konrad stated baldly. "I won't go into any details, but I can put any worries you may have to rest when I assure you that there is absolutely no chance that any cop, journalist, or anyone else, for that matter, will locate us. In short, whatever happens outside, it will have no effect on the day-to-day running of camp. You are all absolutely secure here."

After a few final remarks about the facilities, we were dismissed. Vince had been given the job of clearing the area, and he did this efficiently, chivvying anyone who seemed inclined to linger in the direction of the exit.

Poor Rob didn't need Vince's encouragement to leave, and I solicitously helped him out into the darkness. Joyce was standing just outside, handing out slim little flashlights with the illumination muted by red glass, just like the one Siobhan had been using.

"Thank you, Joyce," I said in my most pleasant tone. It was all very well to have Vince and Mokhtar as adversaries, but it would be stupid to add to the total of potential enemies, so I was going to get on with Joyce if it killed me.

I was thinking about the unfortunate wording of that last thought when Joyce unbent enough to say, "Good night, Dana. Sleep well."

"You too."

The moon was just rising, and although the cloud cover was returning, there was enough light for Rob and me to pick our way to the row of little dwellings without using our red torches. In the moonlight the tents looked charming, just like a collection of small cubby houses.

"I'm third one along from the other end," Rob said, his voice showing his weariness. "Thanks, I'll be okay now."

People were saying good-nights or making their way in the direction of the latrines. We'd all been given the basic information when we arrived: where to get filtered drinking water; where the meals were served; where our beds were; where the showers and toilet facilities were located.

I went back along the row to my tent. It was intriguing to consider what system, if any, had been used to allot the sleeping quarters. While Brit had been reading out the allocations, I'd gone to a lot of trouble to memorize exactly which tent belonged to which person.

There were nine tents in the row — one had obviously been for Tom, who hadn't got past the motel in Darwin, so it was empty. I was at the end closest to the dining area, but farthest from the showers and latrines. A meter and a half away was the spare tent. Then came Forgettable Wade, Evonne, Fergus, Cliff, Rob, Patsy, and, at the other end of the line, Mokhtar.

Earlier, when Brit, touching each person on the shoulder as she allotted his or her tent, had indicated the three occupied by Wade, Evonne, and Cliff, their names had meant nothing to me. Grinning, I now thought how appropriate it was that Fergus and Evonne's quarters were next to each other, and not too close to me.

Inside, I lit my lamp, and with judicious use of my mug and water bottle, I cleaned my teeth while sitting on the narrow stretcher bed. Never had a basin and running water seemed more luxurious — even the shabby little bathroom in the Darwin motel had been a palace compared to this.

Laughing to myself about my pioneer spirit, I climbed out through the flap into the night air for a visit to the latrines. Although clouds whipped across the moon's face, there was still enough light to see reasonably well, although the vegetation cast inky shadows.

On my way back I was overcome with an irresistible impulse to reconnoiter. Everyone seemed to have settled down for the night. No lights, red or otherwise, showed, and all I could hear was the soft crunch of leaf litter under my walking boots, the sigh of a light breeze in the trees, and assorted odd noises from unseen creatures, many of which I imagined were horrifically large insects with lethal bites.

Rather priding my stalking abilities, I drifted around the camp, referring to my mental map of the place as I went. The camp was laid out in a rough rectangle, with our students' row on the east side, opposite to the instructors' tents on the west. The instructors' tents, I was pleased to see, were as tiny as ours. To the north there were two large tents, one of them the dining room–assembly area tent where we'd all just been. Adjoining, the smaller of the two was no doubt the kitchen. Behind them both was the only solid structure in the camp — a prefabricated iron shed painted in camouflage colors. I checked and found it padlocked. Due south were the showers, and past them at a prudent distance, the latrines.

In the middle of the rectangle was the administration tent, and farther south from it were two largish tents. I figured they were probably classrooms, and was investigating them when the moon took the opportunity to duck behind a substantial cloud, and almost total darkness descended.

I was feeling around in my pocket for my red-light torch when a voice said softly behind me, "What are you doing out here?"

In such a situation I'd been trained to go immediately into attack mode, but it was highly unlikely that Dana Wright would have reacted that way, so after what I hoped was only an infinitesimal pause, I exclaimed, "My God! You scared me half to death!"

I fumbled around, convincingly, I hoped, then managed to switch on my flashlight. Its red glow illuminated Siobhan's grim face. As if my hand were shaking, I wavered the beam around enough to see that she held in her left hand a heavy rifle, barrel pointed to the ground. I'd observed earlier that she was right-handed, so this was reassuring — she didn't intend to shoot me, at least not at the moment.

On a strap around her neck hung lightweight night glasses. A glance assured me that they were an advanced model.

I silently cursed my stupidity. All the time I had been congratulating myself that I was doing a skillful scrutiny of the area under cover of darkness, Siobhan had been able to watch me, using a technology that made night as clear as day.

"Well?" said Siobhan. "I asked what you were doing."

"Basically snooping," I said. "I didn't feel sleepy, so I thought I'd look around."

She hefted the rifle. "I could have shot you."

"Would you have?"

She smiled slightly. "Possibly."

"I've explained why I'm here, but why are *you* wandering around in the dark?" I made my tone friendly, confiding, and just a little intimate — the last I couldn't resist, under the circumstances.

"I'm on guard duty."

Again, I could have kicked myself. I was getting seriously slack, and it worried me. I should have automatically taken into consideration the fact that Edification was likely to roster guards at night.

"That's a bit paranoid," I said. "We're in the middle of nowhere."

"Survival is being extra careful."

She could say that again.

The cloud cover over the moon thinned, and a faint silver light permeated the gloom. "I'll walk you back to your tent," Siobhan said.

We went in silence, the whispers of the night swirling seductively around me. She was gorgeous, and probably straight as a ruler. Pity.

When we reached my little dwelling, I said lightly, "I'd ask you in, but I guess you have to stay on duty."

She nodded, then, turning away, said so softly that I almost didn't hear it, "Another time, perhaps."

CHAPTER THIRTEEN

"Attention, please!"

Conversation over breakfast slowly died down, until only Patsy's voice could be heard saying, ". . . not what I'd call a proper breakfast. Start your day with bacon and eggs, that's what I say."

I'd decided that Patsy's voice was like the woman herself, comfortably assured, but underneath there was a thread of vitriol.

Joyce, who had climbed onto a bench so she could

be clearly seen, gave Patsy a thin smile. "I'm glad you brought up that subject, Patsy."

Patsy said heartily, "I bet you are."

Joyce was wearing a voluminous khaki smock, far too large for her thin body. She swept the room with an all-encompassing look, then declared, "You are not here to eat gourmet food, but to learn to be warriors."

This last word seemed to please her, because her hollow face flushed a little as she repeated, "Warriors! Warriors in the service of whatever cause you believe in enough to die for."

"I'm not dying for nobody," declared Evonne, her square face truculent. She shook her heavy head until her long ringlets bounced. "Or nothin'."

Joyce's lips tightened. She continued in a much more moderate tone. "It's not possible to use the generator, except in emergencies, because of the noise it makes, so we have a refrigerator run on kerosene. Space in it is very limited, and we don't have a separate freezer, so Corrina and Aaron use a lot of dehydrated food, canned stuff, and the like. They do make bread in a camp oven every day, but otherwise they are limited in what they can provide for you. I must assure you every meal is nutritious, and we have taken individual dietary restrictions into account."

"I liked my breakfast," said Cliff stoutly. When everyone looked at him, his freckled face went a deep red. He added defiantly, "Well, I did."

I hadn't minded breakfast either. The reconstituted powered milk in my coffee had been a bit hard to take, but the muesli was fine with it, and I noticed that Wade, who was sitting next to me, had gobbled up his porridge with enthusiasm.

"I happen to think," said Joyce, looking militant, "that Corrina and Aaron do a fine job under difficult circumstances. If anyone has any complaints, he or she is welcome to take over the cooking."

She glared at Patsy, who had assumed a type of Buddha-like but mocking expression that I regarded with admiration. I'd always found it difficult to look sagacious and sarcastic at the same time.

Joyce indicated the moon face of a large clock that had been attached high up on one canvas wall. "Please synchronize your watches with the time shown there. You will be expected back here in precisely twenty minutes."

"*Sieg heil,*" said Rob sardonically. He was still very pale, but he insisted that his headache had gone, and that as the day went on he would feel better and better. I had my doubts, as his hands had a tremor and he'd hardly eaten a mouthful of breakfast.

Twenty minutes later we were all back, and Gary took the floor to cover safety issues. His pale hair was still wet from a shower, and his face was red raw, presumably from a close shave. He scratched absently at the flaking skin on the back of one hand as he began, "There are many physical perils here in the Kimberleys — treacherous terrain, poisonous snakes and spiders, et cetera, et cetera, but the greatest danger is from an unexpected direction."

Fergus elbowed me. "Danger's a bit of spice, eh? Makes life worth living." His grin widened. "Like, I'm a bit dangerous, in an exciting sort of way."

I smothered a laugh. "You are?"

His smile disappeared. "Don't you write me off," he said.

At the front, Gary was warming up. "Okay, I'd like

you to point at the person nearest to you. Look them directly in the eyes. That person is your second greatest danger." He paused for that to sink in, and to allow the smirks and smart comments to abate. "Okay, now turn your hand so your finger points at yourself. Think about it. That's right! *You* are the greatest danger to your own welfare."

"This is pop psychology," said Mokhtar, his voice scathing. His slim body was vibrating with anger. "If this is the standard Edification reaches, I'd be better off somewhere else."

Gary gave him a feral grin. "Oh yeah? I can show you facts and figures. Most serious accidents are caused by human error. Taking unacceptable risks, not looking where you're going, being careless with weapons —" He broke off to stare meaningfully at Mokhtar. "And thinking you know it all. *Hubris*, it's called. If you need me to translate, that's excessive, dangerous pride. Want to comment?"

Mokhtar's face was hard with contained anger, but he held his tongue.

After a tension-filled moment, Gary continued as though Mokhtar hadn't spoken. "Now, a comment about the terrain. Konrad's already mentioned that you should be careful, but I'm going to advise you to have eyes in the back of your head. The rock we're standing on is sandstone, marvelous for picturesque gorges because it's easily carved by the forces of weather — by rivers and steams and the drip, drip, drip of rain. But that makes it deceptive, too. The rock will seem solid, but that can be an illusion. Don't go close to the edge of cliffs — the edge may crumble and pitch you into the depths. Don't trust that the rock face you intend to climb will hold. And there are many picturesque waterfalls that will tempt you to come closer. Don't get too close, or you may find yourself part of the ecosystem in a way you didn't intend."

Gary smiled as several people chuckled at this comment. "Okay, a couple more things to watch out for. First, snakes. Australia has some of the deadliest in the world, but dealing with them is simple once you understand that they are more afraid of you than you are of them. Don't attack them, don't try to scare them, don't get in the way when they try to escape. Live and let live is the way to go."

"What about spiders?" Evonne's face was screwed up with extreme distaste. "Jesus, I hate the buggers."

I saw Brit, sitting at the back, nodding a vigorous agreement to this sentiment.

"Spiders, centipedes, various biting insects — avoid them," commanded Gary. "Shake out your boots every morning. Check your clothes before you put them on. Never, ever put your fingers in anything that a spider or the like can hide in."

He put up his hands as several people began asking questions. "Later you can ask anything you like. Right now Vince will be talking to you about crocodiles, and I'd advise you to listen carefully. He's an expert."

Lipless Vince an expert? I didn't have a high opinion of his intelligence, so I found that hard to believe. I watched him get to his feet, his black eyes emotionless, his arms hanging loose at his sides. Definitely an android.

Vince cleared his throat and began in his thin voice, "Camp E is closer to the ocean than you realize. The stream to the north of us forms a waterfall that runs down a cliff into saltwater — a channel that runs directly to the sea."

"Can we go fishing?" asked Wade.

I saw the first genuine amusement that Vince had ever shown when I'd been watching. "Fishing?" he said. "You'll be the bait, mate!"

"Crocodiles," announced Patsy with authority. "Des and I heard all about them on our Kimberley tour. Mean bastards, that'll snap you in two."

Ignoring Patsy's contribution, Vince said, as though reading it from an invisible text, "Australia has two types of crocodile. The smaller freshwater crocodile, also called the Johnston crocodile, has a long snout and is harmless to humans. The one you have to worry about is the saltwater or estuarine crocodile, found in the sea, rivers, and inlets all over northern Australia. Males grow to over eight meters long — that's twenty-six feet of killing machine."

"So we treat them like snakes, and don't go near them." Fergus looked around for commendation. "That's how I'd handle them."

Showing unexpected animation, Vince said, "These are living dinosaurs — monstrous things that haven't changed in millions of years because they're perfect for the life they lead. Salties are aggressive, unbelievably ferocious, and they lurk in water near the banks of rivers and estuaries, waiting for you to come close enough to grab."

"Oh yeah?" sneered Fergus, who appeared determined to pick a fight with Vince. "You're just trying to scare us with horror stories."

This time Vince did actually smile, and it wasn't a pleasant sight. "Fergus," he said, "let me describe for

115

you what will happen. The croc will be waiting, completely submerged, near the shore or under a river bank, and you, its dinner, will come wandering along, thinking because you can't see anything, you're safe. But salties are patient, they can wait for days, hidden in the murky water. It senses you're close by, and it gets ready to attack..."

Vince had dropped his voice to almost a whisper, and, looking around, I could see that everyone, including Fergus, was hanging on his next words.

"In a split second, Fergus, it's out of the water, and it's got you! You're screaming, caught between its jaws. Have you seen a croc's teeth? You won't get away. It seizes you, and it pulls you into the water, and then it does a death roll, thrashing over to break your neck. Doesn't matter to the crocodile if you survive this, or not, because you'll drown anyway."

Vince paused, then said with silky malice, "Now you're not Fergus anymore — you're lunch. It swims away with your limp body between its jaws, and it stores you deep in the water, jammed between rocks, or pushed under a log."

In the pause that followed this description, Vince radiated satisfaction, Fergus seemed rather shaken, and everyone else looked impressed.

"So swimming's off?" I said.

"*You* can swim if you like, Dana," said Vince with a malicious grin.

Vince was followed by Gary, who took us through the topography of the immediate area — a plateau of sandstone, featuring eucalyptus forest in open woodland with small patches of rain forest at the margins. He gave us a map of the camp's surroundings and advised us of the hazards. At ten-thirty we broke for

116

refreshments. We had free time then until half past eleven, when we were to enroll in appropriate classes.

Brit sought me out. "Can I have a word?"

I followed her outside into a welcome breeze. There'd been a few splatters of rain during the night, but the morning had been fine so far. "What's up?"

Brit patted my shoulder consolingly. "I'm sorry about Vince. It was uncalled what he said to you, even though you should have realized you can't swim near saltwater crocodiles."

"I was joking."

"Oh? Well . . ."

"Vince doesn't like me." I was stating the obvious.

"He doesn't like women in general," said Brit. "Particularly strong women who have opinions and aren't afraid to give them."

"That would be me."

Brit flashed her winsome smile. "It certainly would be. Just don't take Vince personally. I mean, he doesn't like *me*." Her tone indicated that this was an extraordinary failing on Vince's part.

Now was the time to start earning my keep. "Brit," I said, "I've been wondering why someone like you joined Edification. I mean, there are so many other places where I can see you using your skills to great advantage."

Flattery was a tried-and-true technique, and it didn't fail me here.

"You're very perceptive," said Brit, tapping me on the arm. "I thought so, the moment we met."

I spread my hands in that potent trust-me gesture that used-car salespeople employ to such good effect. "You know my history," I declared, "but I don't know anything about what made you a radical activist. In

117

my case it was the influence of my parents' beliefs. Was it like that for you?"

"Animals," said Brit, surprising me. "I love animals much more than people. I always have."

"I like them too."

My contribution to the conversation was only to keep Brit talking, and she obediently went on, "Vivisection. I can't even bear to think about it." Her expression became bleakly determined. "Anyone who hurts an animal, especially using scientific research as an excuse, should die."

Death was a little extreme, but I agreed wholeheartedly with her view in general. "They're monsters," I said, nodding sympathetically. "Have you been personally involved in protests?"

"Protests?" said Brit with scorn. "They're not effective, Dana. *Action* is. That's why I support Edification. We teach people how to take the law into their own hands." Her eyes flashed with righteous fire. "We show them techniques, strategies, that strike right at the heart of the establishment."

"How does this help animal welfare?"

Brit was off and running. "Some of it doesn't, of course, but most radical movements are aimed at the corrupt heart of government and the drug companies and universities and the military that all carry out unspeakable outrages against defenseless creatures . . ." She took a breath. "Oh, and people too, of course."

"Sorry to interrupt," said Konrad, his expression serious, "but we have some news." Joyce stood beside him, hands linked in front of her khaki smock.

Brit subsided, the passion draining out of her face. "What about?"

Konrad spoke to me. "It's your brother."

I had the sudden hope that Norbert had been caught, or even killed. "Did he make it into Australia?"

"He's in the country."

Joyce chimed in with, "He was smart, and didn't come direct. A high-quality fake passport got him into New Zealand, then he took a flight to Brisbane, and fooled them there, too."

I experienced the now familiar sinking feeling. "How do you know this?"

"It's all over the news — we picked it up on several channels," said Konrad. "Your brother was just one step ahead of them. Information from London giving the name he'd taken arrived just after he cleared customs in Brisbane."

Brit looked at my face, then said bracingly, "The situation hasn't changed. This guy still doesn't know where Dana is, so he's no closer than before. And it's only a matter of time until he's caught. He can't run forever."

The others nodded agreement. I didn't say anything. It was as if some implacable machine was after me, and no matter what I did or said, Norbert Cummins would inevitably find me.

CHAPTER FOURTEEN

When I told Brit that I'd promised to help Siobhan collate and staple class materials, she volunteered to walk me to the admin. tent. She was cheered by our shared outrage over animal cruelty, so I took the opportunity that her sunny view of me presented to try a little information-gathering.

In a confidential, between-us-girls manner, I said, "Brit, I'm puzzled by something, and I wonder if you could tell me what you think."

Personally, I always found it gratifying to be asked

my opinion, and clearly so did Brit. "Yes?" she said, her face open. "What do you want to know?"

"Well, frankly, it's to do with Joyce." I glanced around, then dropped my voice. "I hope I'm not speaking out of turn, but last night Gary warned me to be careful as far as Joyce was concerned. I just wondered exactly what he meant, and if it has anything to do with Siobhan, because Joyce seemed . . ." I waved my hand in an inconclusive gesture.

I added earnestly, "This Edification course is very important to me, Brit, and I don't want to put a foot wrong."

I almost felt a pang of guilt, it was so easy. Brit halted, put a confiding hand on my elbow, and shook her head ruefully. "It's a shame, Dana, it really is, but Joyce is her own worst enemy, know what I mean? She's had a thing for Siobhan for some time."

"You mean something sexual? Siobhan *is* very attractive." I did my best to make this sound like a cool, unbiased observation.

Brit blushed slightly. I recalled the exchange in the kitchen in Sydney, where Joyce had made an obliquely mocking reference to Brit and Siobhan.

"I think there is an element of that," said Brit, "but mainly, I believe it's professional jealousy."

"Oh?"

"Joyce was one of the founding members of Edification, along with Konrad. We're supposed to all be equals, but" — she paused to send me a meaningful look — "like they say, some are more equal than others."

"*Animal Farm.*"

"What?"

"That's where that quote comes from, about being more equal. George Orwell's *Animal Farm*."

As Brit blinked at the change of subject I made a mental note to resist showing off. "You mentioned professional jealousy . . . ?"

"Siobhan's a relative newcomer. She has a wonderful history in anarchist movements, particularly on the Continent. She speaks several languages, you know." This last comment was delivered in tones of deep admiration.

Hey, I could have said, *I speak several languages myself*. But of course I couldn't mention my facility with Indonesian and Japanese. Dana Wright spoke French and a little German, and had never had anything to do with Asian cultures.

I could have happily discussed Siobhan more, but I forced myself back to the topic at hand. "But that doesn't explain what Gary meant when he warned me about Joyce."

Brit released my elbow, and we began walking again. "To be blunt," she said, wrinkling her nose, "Joyce is rather indiscriminate. Each new course she picks a likely target, usually a woman, and puts the hard word on her."

"She's indiscriminate?" I repeated. "And I'm a likely target? Well, thanks, Brit!"

"You know what I mean." She chuckled at my mock outrage. "Look at the choice — there's you, Patsy, and Evonne. I know who'd I'd go for."

"Me?"

Brit put her arm around my waist and gave me a squeeze. "No contest."

I couldn't detect anything sexual in her comradely embrace. I said, friend to friend, "So help me here.

I'm not walking into a minefield am I? There's never been anything between Joyce and Siobhan?"

Brit's animated face became wooden. "How could there be? Siobhan's straight."

All my instincts wrong? I didn't want to believe it.

"Bit disappointing for Joyce," I remarked, adding mentally, *And maybe for you, too, Brit.*

"Yeah," said Brit, her voice flat.

Siobhan welcomed us with complimentary enthusiasm. "Wonderful! I'm up to my ears here." She grinned at Brit. "Are you going to help as well?"

Brit hesitated, and I could tell she wanted to stay, but she said, "Sorry, I promised Aaron I'd do a stock-take of the supplies."

On her way out she sent a lingering glance back at Siobhan from the tent entrance — Brit apparently couldn't help telegraphing her emotions — but Siobhan seemed quite oblivious.

They would have made a good pair, at least visually. Brit was glossy haired, with even teeth and amber eyes; Siobhan was even more striking, with the high cheekbones that photographers drool over and an indefinable air of being special. And her voice I particularly liked. I hadn't realized before quite how attractive an English accent could be.

"It's good of you to give up your free time," said the object of my thoughts, clearing a space on a trestle table. "I'd have thought, after I interrupted your explorations last night, that you'd want to take this chance to look around in daylight."

"I've already done it. Got up at dawn." With a guileless smile I added, "Apparently there's no threat to the camp early in the morning, as I noticed there was no one on guard duty."

"No one you saw."

She was bluffing. I'd been careful to check, and there'd been no sentry. The whole camp had been snoozing in that strange half-light before sunrise. I'd woken very early, and after abandoning any idea of going back to sleep, I'd got up and, bearing in mind I would be exploring in the bush, had put on long pants to protect my legs, carefully tucking them into my heavy socks, as I feared leeches or worse were waiting for me.

It had been wonderful to be the only one awake as the eastern sky, strewn with a patchwork of clouds, was flooded with a spectacular orange sunrise. Birds stirred, a breeze blew scents of eucalyptus gums, and I could relax and be Denise Cleever, walking in the early light, enjoying everything that impinged on my senses. My boots stirred up scents from the damp ground; everywhere there were sounds of dripping water, twitterings, branches creaking gently. Droplets hung from every leaf, and soon I was drenched as my passage through the undergrowth shook them loose.

I went north, threading my way around gray box, white gums, and other trees and bushes with care, one arm up to collect the filmy spider webs I couldn't avoid. Indeed, spiders seemed to have been very active building webs, and I kept an eye out for any that might be lurking on a branch, ready to drop onto my unprotected head. Good sense told me that would be the last thing a sensible spider would do, but my imagination painted such shocking spider-jumping pictures that I surrendered to the concept that it was a real possibility.

After about twenty minutes I came to a stream.

Fed by the long wet season, it was running fast and deep in the bed it had carved out of the sandstone. Paperbarks growing close to the water shed their sheets of bark in untidy piles. A kingfisher dived into the water, then emerged with a flurry of blue-violet wings, some small thing wriggling in its long beak.

With some difficulty I followed the watercourse, coming eventually to the most spectacular drop. The water leapt the last rocky barriers in its bed and fell straight down in a precipitous drop to froth white in the green water far beneath. I was at the top of a sandstone cliff. Looking over — my stomach did a somersault — I could see huge boulders that had broken away and tumbled down to form a jumbled mass of stone in the water.

I had started back and had been walking about fifteen minutes when something moved near my feet. Visions of snakes zipped through my mind as rapidly as the Olympic standard backward leap I accomplished. I let out my breath in a long sigh when an echidna shuffled into view, his snout vacuuming along the ground as he collected unfortunate ants with his sticky tongue.

My presence hadn't caused the echidna one moment's concern — his spines weren't erect with alarm, nor had he decided to roll into a protective, spiky ball.

"Ant murderer," I said.

That had some effect. He halted and peered shortsightedly in my direction. Apparently deciding I posed no threat, he resumed his amble, stopping every now and then to scratch up the surface of leaf mold with his curved claws to expose some delicacy.

He was so delightful to watch that I had trouble

tearing myself away, so when I got back to the camp I had to go straight to breakfast, even though my clothes were still damp. I didn't mention to anyone where I'd been. I wasn't trying to be secretive, but I wanted to treasure that time apart, where I hadn't had to pretend to be anybody, or to fake belief in precepts that I didn't accept. It was ridiculous, but alone, way out in the bush, I'd said my own name out loud several times. Why, I wasn't altogether sure.

Now I was Dana Wright again, who believed with all her heart and soul that the established systems must be destroyed, using any means available. So dedicated was Dana that neither distance nor considerable financial outlay had prevented her from planning to attend this training camp in one of the remotest parts of Australia's wildernesses.

In my mind I held an image of the real Dana lying comatose in a white bed in a white room. I pictured many devices attached to her unconscious body with various wires and tubes, and, just like a medical drama on TV, a monitor would be beeping monotonously as nurses drifted in and out, checking her condition. Now and then a doctor would appear to test her reflexes and jot something on her chart.

Or perhaps Dana was awake. My mental picture changed to suit this scenario. Now she was sitting up, pale, confused, saying faintly, "What happened? Why am I here? I should be in Australia . . ." And a nurse, really with MI6, was saying soothingly that she must lie down and rest, otherwise she'd never get her strength back.

Even if in reality Dana had regained consciousness, she wouldn't be permitted to leave the hospital or to communicate with the outside world, but would stay under detention until my impersonation was over. It was a matter of British national security, covered by a blanket "D" Notice that would prevent any person from revealing anything to anybody, anytime.

Siobhan jerked me out of my imaginings by handing me a stapler and indicating the pages I was to collate and fasten. We didn't talk. I got into that hypnotic rhythm of work where time seems to stop and the repetition of actions is a calming pleasure. Siobhan had a portable CD player, and the tent was filled with the mesmerizing sounds of Sade. By the time the singer got to the song "Smooth Operator" I had accomplished my task.

"All done," I said. "Anything else?"

"Dana, that's great. Thank you."

I leaned against a table while she stacked handouts in neat piles. On the canvas wall beside me I was amused to notice a schedule that detailed sentry duties. I checked it out, then said to her, "You're on guard again tonight?"

"Why?"

I shrugged. "Just wondering. So how long are you on? Not all night, surely."

Siobhan gave me a half-patient, half-humorous look. "Why is it that I think you're trying to find out the sentry schedule? Could it be for some nefarious reason?"

"Nefarious as hell," I agreed. "And I'm especially helped by the fact that the schedule is right here on the wall."

Siobhan raised her eyebrows. "So it is. How observant of you."

It was clear that one person was on duty each evening from eight to one, and that was all. "You only have patrols at night? Seems strange, as I can't see how anyone could sneak up on us in the pitch-darkness."

"Frankly," said Siobhan, "we're more concerned at what's happening in the camp than worrying about intruders."

"You've had trouble before?"

She shrugged. "A little. Nothing we couldn't handle."

"And the guy who died of snakebite?"

She gave me a chilly smile. "The wonder is, the snake didn't die from biting him."

"A great guy, obviously."

"Thanks for the help, Dana." This topic was obviously closed.

I picked up one of the handouts Siobhan had been assembling. "Interesting to see who's teaching what," I said.

Joyce, I was fascinated to see, would be our bomb expert. I had no trouble imagining her taking great pleasure in destructive explosions. Konrad would be teaching how to manage riots, as well as pointers on efficient assassinations. Brit was an instructor in surveillance and, for some reason a surprise to me, arson. Vince, I thought appropriately, was down for interrogation techniques and also kidnapping. Gary would be covering biological and chemical weapons, and the disruption of vital urban services. Aaron, probably because of his duties in the kitchen, had only ecoterrorism.

And Siobhan? "I see you'll be teaching two classes," I said. "Government Responses to Terrorism — seems a little dry — and Strategies to Panic the Public. Hey, that last gets to me. It's been my ambition to panic the public ever since I was a kid."

"Then perhaps you'd better enroll in the class."

Enrollment! I glanced at my watch. "Yikes, I'll be late if I don't go right now." I threw her my best cheeky grin. "I'd hate to make a bad impression."

She cocked her head, but didn't say anything.

Hurrying to the meeting, I thought that Siobhan was beginning to intrigue me more than was wise. In real life I wasn't unattached — I had a relationship that was strong, but hampered by distance, plus the inconvenient fact that Roanna was still under suspicion for treason, so, as an ASIO employee, I was not supposed to have any contact with her.

I assured myself that anything that might happen with Siobhan would fall under the umbrella of work duties, although in my imagination I could hear Livia chortling at this rationalization.

One thing made it impossible for me to get in too deep with Siobhan — she was a terrorist, and a teacher of terrorism. People had certainly been hurt and possibly died because of her activities.

When I got to the assembly tent, I found I was the last to arrive, and only squeaked in by a second or two before the eleven-thirty deadline. Konrad, waiting at the door, frowned at me. "I've been helping Siobhan," I said hastily, feeling like a kid at school.

"Attention, everyone," said Joyce, who was in charge of enrollments. I could imagine her as an acid-voiced school principal, very strong on discipline for her students, but contemptuous of anything that smacked of wishy-washy, feel-good stuff.

"There are four compulsory classes that everyone

must complete, and then you have a free choice of the other subjects to make up your full program. The compulsory classes are Micro and Macro Management of Riots, Surveillance Techniques, Government Responses to Terrorism, and Attacks on Urban Targets. You are also strongly encouraged to take Advanced Bomb Construction. Those with little experience of explosive devices are advised to start with Simple Bomb Construction. If you have any questions, ask Gary, Konrad, or me for further information."

There was much milling about as we filled in our names for the courses. Rob, who as he'd predicted, was looking much better, conferred with me over Kidnapping.

"I want to do the course because I can see its value for me," he said, "but that bastard Vince is teaching it."

"If you can't hack having to deal with Vince, then forget it," I advised, "but if you really think it'll be useful, then don't let the fact he's the instructor put you off."

I had a moment's appalled thought that I was happily discussing the pros and cons of enrolling in a course that would be teaching the fundamentals of committing an unconscionable crime.

"I'll do it if you do," said Rob.

"Okay," I agreed, extra amiable.

I'd been intending to put myself down for this course anyway, as I was determined to blunt Vince's animosity toward me. This was not for any personal reason, as I disliked the man intensely, but because it would make information-gathering about him much easier if we got on with each other.

When I finished enrolling, apart from the compulsory items, I had followed Joyce's advice and put myself down for both bomb courses and Assassination. I had added Kidnapping, Arson, and Ecoterrorism, and rounded it all off with Strategies to Panic the Public. I was going to be one busy student.

"Before we clear the tent so that Aaron and Corrina can set up for lunch," said Konrad, "I have an important announcement to make that will affect all of you."

This even got the attention of Patsy, whom I'd overheard telling Evonne how her late husband had been "riddled with cancer, just riddled with it ..."

When Konrad was satisfied that everyone was listening, he said, "One of the problems of the training we do here in Camp E is that it's basically theoretical. To overcome this, we've decided to add another element. You will be divided into two teams, and each will prepare to hit a real target in Sydney. This will not just be an exercise — one of the teams will be selected to carry out the strike and achieve the set objective."

"What sort of target?" asked Mokhtar.

"It's open to discussion, but at the moment we're considering a political assassination."

Mokhtar, for once looking pleased, said, "This is excellent. Do we have the opportunity to have some input on the target?"

"What do you have in mind?"

"A Jew," said Mokhtar disdainfully. "That's what I have in mind."

"We'll take your opinion into consideration."

Gary, his face tight, glared at Mokhtar. I was struck by the incongruity of someone like Gary being upset at anti-Semitism while he was cheerfully preparing to teach the efficient use of biological and chemical weapons.

With a final dark look at Mokhtar, Gary turned his attention to the rest of us. "This is a valuable addition to the Edification syllabus that will take each of you right through from the planning stage to the full implementation of the strike, and then the strategies to avoid detection and capture. You will learn essential lessons that can never be taught in a classroom setting."

"What happens afterward?"

Konrad acknowledged Cliff's question with a pleased smile. "Possibly the most valuable part of the exercise. You will be returning here to Camp E for extensive debriefing. We will analyze exactly what went right, what went wrong, and how the strike could be improved."

"When will all this happen?" My voice showed relaxed interest, but inwardly I was close to panic. I was hermetically sealed away from the outside world, so how was I going to alert ASIO that a terrorist attack was planned?

"The timing will depend on the readiness of each team and the availability of a suitable target. The team not chosen for the hit will be deployed to create a diversionary event, probably using smoke bombs and stun grenades. This way the massive law enforcement response to the assassination will be split between two venues. In the confusion and panic it will be much easier for you all to slip away undetected."

I was so tense I would twang if someone touched me. Abruptly my task to infiltrate Edification and identify participants had been superseded by the urgent need to short-circuit this unforeseen terrorist strike.

My mind began to spin with possibilities — maybe I could feign serious illness and be taken outside for medical help. It was more than likely that only one person would take me, and I could deal with him or her once we were away from the camp. Or I could wait until we reached the doctor, and then act. Yes, that would be better, because I wasn't an expert in driving in the challenging road conditions of the Wet.

"One last thing," said Konrad. "Now that you all know that we are going to carry out a real-life sortie, absolute security has to apply. No one will be permitted to break off training and leave the camp for any cause whatsoever. That includes accidents, snakebites, and illness, however serious."

"What if you're dying?" asked Fergus, aggrieved.

"Then you die," said Konrad.

CHAPTER FIFTEEN

After lunch, which was a cold selection of canned ham or Spam — I hadn't had that since I was a child — potato and bean salads, and side dishes of pickled cucumbers and beets, we all trooped off to our first compulsory class, Macro and Micro Management of Riots.

My guess had been right about the two tents in the center of the camp — they were classrooms. We sat four to a bench in one of them, like kids in an old-fashioned country school. In front of each of us was a writing pad and pen. "They must expect us to make notes," Patsy hissed to me. "I don't need to — I've got a photogenic memory."

"Photographic," I corrected.

She frowned at me suspiciously. "What?"

I was saved from answering by Konrad's entrance. He didn't waste time, but launched straight into the topic, starting with an overview, and then using as an illustration the Group of Eight summit of world leaders in Genoa, Italy.

"Genoa is an excellent example of organized anarchy," he said. "There were up to a hundred thousand people protesting globalization. Hidden within that number were two thousand or so anarchists who were formed into specialized groups, each with a specific role."

He took a marker and began drawing a flow chart on a whiteboard set up on an easel.

"Here's how it was organized. Protected from the riot police by the mass of peaceful demonstrators, the anarchists put on masks so they couldn't be identified from media shots. Many also wore motorcycle helmets or construction hard hats. Then the subgroups activated in a set order.

"First came the window-smashers, targeting banks and shops. They were followed by the second group, the looters, who began to ransack the businesses. The police, naturally, converged on the scene, and as they did, the third group, the firebombers, went into action, hurling Molotov cocktails. Simultaneously, the fourth group, stone-throwers, rained a hail of missiles on the riot police. Incidentally, the stones, ripped up from the street, or smashed off building facades with hammers, were collected for ease of use in shopping carts taken from the looted stores."

Cliff put a hand up for attention, but Konrad said, "Questions later, unless it's a vital one." Apparently it wasn't, as Cliff subsided, looking rather miffed.

Konrad resumed. "Similar techniques were used over and over, with small numbers of anarchists joining larger groups of protest marchers, and then provoking the police into violent confrontations. The police had rubber bullets, tear gas, armored personnel carriers, water cannons, and live ammunition. The anarchists had tight organization, simple weapons, and the ability to strike and then slip away to join the crowds of peaceful demonstrators."

He scribbled furiously on the whiteboard, then stood back for us to see what he had written: *Violence is central to the media's attention. Unless things get smashed, nobody pays attention.*

"Many newspapers reported this quote from an anonymous English anarchist. It sums up a very important lesson that you all must learn: if there is no publicity, then there is no point. Noise, commotion, violent action that makes for good television is vital. Work on this, be creative, put on a good show." He grinned. "Build a riot, and they will come."

Cliff had his hand up again. Irritated, Konrad said, "Yes?"

"Killing a world leader would get terrific publicity. Did any of the anarchists get close to doing this?"

"No, and they didn't expect to because the security was too tight, but they did attack the ring of riot police protecting the venue by using techniques taken from crowd control. Standing shoulder to shoulder, lines of anarchists holding plastic shields charged the ranks protecting the building."

As Konrad went on to discuss the important role

that the Internet now played in the organization of riots, my thoughts wandered, although I kept an attentive expression on my face, a talent I'd developed from long practice at boring ASIO meetings.

How was I going to get a message out? Feigning serious illness was obviously not going to work. I'd try to get a look at the ham radio in the admin. tent, but I wasn't sanguine about raising anybody on it who would be of help. If we'd known about the radio ASIO would have arranged to monitor the bandwidths, but as that wasn't happening, I didn't have a lot of faith that I'd manage to contact a ham radio operator who'd believe one word about a terrorist plot.

This morning's walk had convinced me that there was no way I could get out of the area on foot, and even if I did make it to the Kalumburu Road, while I was trying to thumb a ride Edification could pick me up as easily as any passerby.

One of the Toyota four-wheel drives presented the best possibility. Covered with camouflage netting, the three vehicles were parked under a huge gum tree at the end of the almost imperceptible track we had taken in to the camp. I'd disable two, take the one with the most fuel, and make a bolt for civilization and a telephone, praying I didn't get stuck in a mud-hole on the way.

If all else failed, I could wait until we were out of the Kimberleys and on the way to accomplish our practical lesson in terrorism, and by one means or the other make sure that the strike didn't succeed. This was, necessarily, the last resort.

The details might be fuzzy, and luck would play a large part, but I felt some comfort that I had at least two possible ways to foil the planned assassination.

After our lesson on riots we had a twenty-minute break for refreshments. I was thirsty, so I didn't stand around chatting, but trotted straight over to the main assembly tent. Inside, Gary was just taping a sheet to the wall.

"Want to see who's in your group?" he asked.

I glanced at it. "*Fergus?* Fair go, can't I have Rob instead?"

There were two teams, Orange and Yellow. The Orange Team was composed of me, Evonne, Wade, and Fergus. The Yellow Team was Patsy, Mokhtar, Cliff, and Rob.

"Sorry," said Gary, not looking the slightest sorry, "but we've matched you up as far as personalities and skills are concerned. No changes."

I opened my mouth to argue, but the object of my ire, Fergus, came into the tent. "Ah," he said, examining the notice, "I'm in a group with you, Dana. How about that?"

"How about that."

His smile had a touch of malice as he said, "Pity you didn't get your boyfriend in your group."

"My what?"

"Rob. I saw you last night, very lovey-dovey."

I sighed. "Rob had a migraine. I was helping him to his tent." Over Fergus's shoulder I saw that Gary was listening to our conversation with interest.

Fergus nodded knowingly. "Tonight," he announced, "I plan to have a migraine. Would you help me to my tent too?"

"Of course. I'm an equal opportunity helper, although I rather thought you might prefer Evonne."

I saw Gary smile, and realized that Joyce had told

him about my wickedness in sending Evonne to entertain Fergus.

"Here comes your female competition," said Fergus, smirking as Patsy and Evonne entered. He leaned closer to confide, "You're the pick of the bunch, Dana."

"Gosh, thanks."

"A looker like you with a guy like Rob . . ." He shook his head. "You can do better."

"Is 'better' you, Fergus?"

"Too right it is!"

I had to smile at his uncomplicated, peacock self-regard.

The second period of the afternoon was devoted to electives: Gary was teaching Biological Weapons, and Vince was starting his Kidnapping class.

There were four of us enrolled in Kidnapping: me, Rob, Evonne, and Mokhtar. We would have all fitted quite comfortably on one bench, but Mokhtar ostentatiously sat by himself. His pains to be exclusive were of no avail, however, because as soon as Vince came in he demanded that Mokhtar sit with us. "I want you all together where I can see you easily."

It was pleasing to see Mokhtar's dilemma. He would rather die, I was sure, than sit by me, and Evonne was a female too, so she was out. Rob would have to be the buffer between us and him, but Rob was on the very end of the bench, with me next.

"I cannot sit next to a woman," he finally declared.

Vince was clearly not in a mood to pamper anyone. "Sit down, you stupid bastard."

"You'll have to move along," said Mokhtar, pointing at Rob. I smiled to myself as we all made a big deal of shifting to accommodate a now white-with-rage Mokhtar. This was quite fun, I thought, in a strange, twisted sort of way.

Unlike Konrad, who seemed to enjoy teaching, Vince glowered as he looked us over, then began in a monotone that suited, I thought, his robotic self. He ran through the salient points of a successful kidnapping, being careful to refer to the victim as "the subject."

In his introductory remarks Vince rapidly covered the importance of thorough preparation, including the selection of the hiding place for the subject, the smooth accomplishment of the snatch, the process of conveying demands, the tricky concept of juggling the release of the kidnap subject and the simultaneous receipt of whatever it was that one hoped to get, all this without being arrested or killed.

Vince pointed out that many of the kidnappings we were likely to be involved with might not have the payment of money as the desired outcome, but possibly the release of a political prisoner, or the change of a company's or government's policy over some vital matter. "But money never hurts," he added. "I'd always advise asking for a substantial ransom."

"Why not kill the subject immediately?" asked Mokhtar. "Isn't it much simpler to avoid the problem of hiding and guarding the victim, et cetera?"

"Comments?" said Vince. "Rob, what do you think?"

Startled to be asked, Rob's pasty face went pink. "Um," he said. Vince tapped an impatient foot. Rob cleared his throat. "Well, I suppose I think you have to prove the subject is alive, or there's no reason for the ransom to be paid, is there?"

Mokhtar gave a contemptuous snort. "That can be faked. And screams of torture can be taped before the killing. They make a good incentive for payment."

I'd never thought Vince would be an innovative instructor, so I was surprised when he said, "We're going to role-play over the next few days to examine various issues that will be raised today."

Evonne wriggled her thick shoulders. "Don't like role-play," she said. "Waste of time when we could be learning properlike."

"I think we should try one right now." Vince's tone didn't invite discussion. "Okay, here's the situation. It's at the point in the kidnapping where the subject has been snatched, but no ransom has yet been requested."

Pointing at each of us in turn, he said, "Dana, you're the kidnapper, Mokhtar, you're the subject, Evonne, you're the mark who wants the subject back unharmed, and you, Rob, play the cop called in to solve the crime. Okay, position yourselves around the tent."

I sat Mokhtar down on a folding chair in one corner, while Evonne and Rob went to the one diagonally opposite. "Ready?" said Vince. "Okay, we're at the point where Dana makes the first ransom demand."

Mokhtar was unhappy. "I would rather play the kidnapper. Dana can be the subject."

"Just get on with it."

I picked up an imaginary phone and began to punch numbers into it. "Hello," I said. "I've got something you want."

The interaction that followed was, to my astonishment, hilarious. Even Vince's thin mouth curved into the semblance of a smile as I acted out a series of phone calls where I repeated my demands of a million dollars for Mokhtar. Evonne demurred at the amount, making the insulting implication that he wasn't worth that much, and Rob kept repeating, "Keep her talking, we're trying to get a trace."

When Mokhtar, as the subject, became verbally abusive, I put an imaginary bag over his head. Then, when he still wouldn't shut up, I shot him. Naturally, being Mokhtar, he wouldn't die, so I suggested to no one in particular that a mallet and a wooden shaft would not go astray.

By that time everyone except the kidnapping subject was laughing.

Vince then surprised me further by skillfully analyzing what we had been doing in this one element of the operation, detailing the mistakes each of us had made and the reason that this particular kidnapping would be deemed amateur and unlikely to succeed.

At the end of the class we straggled outside to find that there was a light rain falling. Waiting until the others had gone ahead, Vince said to me approvingly, "That was very funny, Dana. And that little prick deserves everything he gets, anyway."

I positively basked in this approbation from such an unlikely source. "Any time," I said. "Do you think *anyone* likes Mokhtar?"

"Good-looking little bastard like that, you'd think he'd be a hit with the ladies."

"Not this lady."

Vince positively confounded me by saying in an almost playful tone, "Lady? I would have taken you for a woman, any day."

I stared after him as he strode off through the rain. Should I worry that he was being pleasant for a change? I didn't flatter myself that my glowing personality had won him over so easily.

That evening it became clear there wasn't going to be much spare time in our daily schedules, as apart from classes, each of us was allocated a set of chores to do. I ended up with recycling cans and bottles — I was to flatten the cans with a neat crushing machine, and smash the bottles to pieces so they'd take up less room in storage. I was quite pleased with the chore I'd drawn when I discovered that poor Cliff was a garbage-sorter, responsible for separating everything for disposal. His tasks included burning flammable rubbish in one of the heavy metal stoves in the kitchen, and burying all organic matter in a deep pit outside the camp area. Plastics and other environmentally unsound materials were to be collected in garden bags and stored for later removal.

After dinner there was a short break, then Brit introduced Surveillance Techniques, one of the three compulsory courses. If there was one thing I fancied myself an expert in, it was surveillance, so I let Brit's words wash over me, half hearing her mention audio bugging, night-vision equipment, infrared illuminators, spy cams, and tracking equipment, both personal and vehicle.

I noticed that all the seven instructors were present. Surely this was not because of Brit's lecture style, although I had to admit she was very vivacious, and followed the teaching manual in trying to make eye contact with every member of her audience. She also smiled a lot, tossed her head, and generally gave the impression that she welcomed this opportunity to bask in a leadership role.

There had to be another reason for this full instructor attendance, but I couldn't imagine what it might be. Whatever it was, it didn't please Joyce, who seemed to be nursing a case of indigestible cold fury. She sat apart from everyone else, her angular body stiff, her eyes dark slits.

My attention went back to Brit, who had moved on to the subject of countersurveillance, and was running through the basic security measures to keep telephones, fax machines, and computers safe.

There was nothing I didn't know backward, so I glanced around at my fellow students. Patsy had retrieved something edible from her bag and was chewing thoughtfully; Wade and Mokhtar were both listening closely — or looked as if they were; Fergus had the glazed expression of one not hearing a word; Evonne had lifted her hair away from her thick neck with one pudgy hand, and was fanning ineffectually with the other; Rob was resting his chin on his palm and appeared about to go to sleep; Cliff was inspecting the canvas ceiling.

I looked to see what had caught his attention, and smiled to see that it was a couple of geckos playing chasings. They were delightful little things, and I'd always thought they had well-developed senses of humor. If so, this was about to be tested.

"Arrgh!" Evonne was on her feet, pointing. "Lizards! Get 'em out!" She made a wild swipe with her writing pad, and they skittered out of reach.

Brit's smile had slipped as everyone's attention went to Evonne, then up to the source of her angst. "People," Brit said, flapping her hands. "People?"

"Jesus, Evonne," snapped Gary, his face red, "they're only bloody geckos. Have you any idea what's crawling around outside, right now?"

"No, I don't. And I don't want to know."

Gary seemed about to run through the hazardous possibilities in unsettling detail, but Konrad silenced him with a shake of his head, then said, "I think Brit's pretty well finished her preliminary remarks, so I'll take this opportunity to give you some new information about your teams."

"But . . ." said Brit, who obviously intended to finish her lecture. "I haven't covered —"

Konrad talked right over her. "We've discussed the matter and decided that each of you would benefit from having a mentor in the preparation for the real-life exercise."

He took a folded page from the top pocket of his shirt as he continued, smiling, "I want you to know that we had quite a task deciding which instructor would be best matched with each person, and we did fight over some of you."

"I reckon the fight might have been over who *not* to get," observed Patsy. The ripple of laughter that this evoked pleased her, and she looked around triumphantly.

"Here's the final list," said Konrad, opening up the page.

Jeez, I thought, don't give me Vince, even if he

was nice this afternoon. And not Joyce, too intense. And not, please God, Brit — I'd strangle her.

"As we have seven instructors and eight students, one instructor has to double up. Fortunately this isn't a problem, as Wade has already had firsthand experience in an assassination, so he won't need quite as much guidance as the rest of you."

We all looked at Wade, who seemed a little embarrassed to be singled out this way.

Konrad waited until our eyes were turned back to him before continuing. "It goes like this: Vince is mentor for both Wade and Cliff, Aaron for Evonne, Brit for Rob, myself for Mokhtar, Siobhan for Dana, Joyce for Patsy, and Gary for Fergus. Now, I'd like you to take this opportunity to talk to your mentors."

"Wow, what a relief," I confessed to Siobhan a few moments later when we had all obediently gone to our mentors. "I felt I was sure to be given in bondage to Vince."

Her faintly Asian features amused, she said, "Actually, I believe it was Joyce who lobbied hardest for the pleasure of your company."

"And you won."

Her slow smile made me tingle. "That depends," she said, "on how you perform."

CHAPTER SIXTEEN

We were kissing. I was on fire. "More," I said urgently. "Much more."

Then I was blinking awake all alone on my narrow stretcher bed. The dream still remained in tantalizing shreds, and I closed my eyes and tried to keep it alive. Like all dreams, it shivered, faded, and was gone.

"I dreamed of kissing you, Siobhan," I whispered to the sloping green wall of my tent. "Did you dream that too?"

I gathered my things and bent double to back out

of my cramped sleeping place. At home I usually showered at night, but standing in the bush in darkness inside a wet canvas cubicle didn't have much appeal, especially as my imagination populated the place with scorpions and trapdoor spiders and snakes and centipedes, every one of them intent on doing me harm.

I looked down the row of tents. Each entrance flap was tightly closed. From the far end came the faint sound of snoring. Probably Patsy. I blessed the fact that my tent was at this end.

Showering early, before anyone else was up and about, had its own special rewards. It was a fine, private time, with the "*chi chi*" of galahs, the beautiful flute-like song of butcherbirds and the sun blossoming on the horizon as the day stretched itself awake. I took a bucket and filled the bush shower with water from the storage tank — cold, of course — and stripped off. There was something delightful about being able to look up and see the sky. It was already warm, and would hit thirty-five degrees Celsius later in the day.

Yesterday Fergus had demanded to know what the real temperature was — by that he meant Fahrenheit — and had endured with good grace the mockery of decimal citizens like me. "About nine-five in your scale," Konrad had said. "And humid, very humid."

I reckoned that by Fergus's standards it was already in the eighties. I toweled myself dry, put on a fresh set of cotton shorts and shirt, stood on one foot and then the other to put on my socks and boots, and emerged, clean and refreshed, into the new day.

Out of the corner of my eye I caught a movement. A thought flashed like fire across my mind. *Norbert*? I dropped my towel and swung around, automatically taking combat position.

"Whoa!" said Aaron. "Steady on, it's me."

"You startled me," I said superfluously.

Even this early, a cigarette drooped from his bottom lip. Its tip burned ruby red as he sucked in a lungful of nicotine. The smoke dribbled through his lazy smile. "Sorry. I wanted to get you alone."

He suddenly guffawed. "Shit, that didn't sound so good. What I meant was, I need to warn you of something."

I picked up my muddy towel and examined it. "Look what you made me do."

"Shocking. I should be thrashed."

I laughed, at the same time thinking how easy it was to forget the evil in people when you interacted with them day by day. Aaron promoted terrorism. He taught people how to maim and kill, how to destroy lives and property, but even so, on a personal level it was fun to indulge in lighthearted verbal sparring with him.

"Have you been lurking outside my shower?" I said severely.

"Guilty as charged, but I had a good reason." His smile faded. "It's to warn you . . . about Joyce."

"About Joyce? Are you serious?"

"Very." He removed the cigarette from his lip and examined it as though surprised to find it there. "Joyce has always been a bit . . . strange. She takes these sudden likes and dislikes."

"Joyce doesn't like me?"

Aaron grinned at my injured tone. "I'm afraid she does like you, and that's the problem." He sobered to add, "Look, don't think I'm talking a load of bull, here, Dana. Joyce is obsessive, and she can be dangerous. She was one of the founders of Edification, and she doesn't like the way that Siobhan, who's only been with us three years, has got so far in the organization."

"I don't see what this has to do with me."

"Joyce was determined to be your mentor, because it would bring her up close and personal with you." He gave a little smirk. "If you see what I mean."

"I see what you mean. But so?"

"Siobhan said she'd prefer to mentor you. This didn't go well with Joyce, and she was even more furious when most of us sided with Siobhan."

"I can see that Joyce might be put out not to get me," I said cheerfully, "but her problem's with Siobhan. Why aren't you warning her?"

"Let me tell you a little story. Something very like this happened at the last training camp. There was a student Joyce particularly took a fancy to, a Korean girl about twenty. The girl pissed Joyce off, and made a line for Konrad instead. So you know what happened?"

"I'm sure you're going to tell me."

"You're doing Simple Bomb Construction with Joyce, I believe. This girl was, too — and one of those simple little bombs went off in her hand. She lost three fingers and most of her thumb."

I stared at him, aghast. "Are you telling me that Joyce deliberately —"

"Too right, I am. So watch out, Dana." He put a hand out and patted my cheek. "I'd hate anything like that to happen to you."

Aaron's warning echoed in my head all through breakfast, Aaron's ecoterrorism lesson, and Brit's expert take on arson.

Lunch was interesting.

"What are these?" Wade asked, poking at the contents of his plate.

I'd deliberately seated myself next to him, so I took this opportunity to be friendly and acquaint him with the sterling qualities of Cornish pasties.

"I don't know about this," he said doubtfully, prodding the fat, shapeless mound of pastry with his fork.

"Don't go by looks. It's delicious." I was exaggerating. I'd sampled some, and it wasn't actually delicious, but it was okay. Of course, I did pride myself on making possibly the best Cornish pasties in the world, so my standards were rather high.

I waited until he had a mouthful, swallowed it, said, "Not too bad, I suppose," and started to chew his next helping before I gushed,

"I'm so happy we're on the same team."

Wade's expression showed surprise, and some measure of gratification. I thought that as a kid he would have been the sort of easily ignored one, who got picked last for sides in sports.

"I hope *our* team is the one chosen to carry out the strike," I burbled.

Wade's nondescript face became quite animated, saying, "Yeah, it's a real charge. Killing someone, I mean. Like when all that planning, and practicing until you've got it right, goes off like clockwork. What a payoff!"

"Tell me," I said, enthusiasm itself.

Wade needed no further encouragement. I was familiar with the crime, which had been the assassination of a high-ranking Malaysian politician twelve months earlier. And Wade was right when he said it had gone like clockwork. The killing had been fast and efficient, and no one had been arrested.

I couldn't ask specific questions about his fellow conspirators, but as he talked I concentrated on storing away every detail he revealed. Later that information would help identify both Wade and those who had carried out the murder with him.

I was so intent I forgot for a moment that my first class of the afternoon was Simple Bomb Construction with Joyce.

"This will be a practical course," Joyce announced, hands on her narrow hips, "but naturally, because of the noise generated by larger explosions, we will stick to small charges."

Everyone but Mokhtar and Wade had joined the class. Fergus said to me in a low voice, "I really know all about bombs, but thought a refresher course couldn't hurt."

"Wise, really."

He checked to see if this was a serious remark. Reassured, he said, "Better safe than sorry."

I could win a duel of clichés. "Nothing ventured, nothing gained."

Fergus was puzzling over that when Joyce snapped, "Please pay attention!" She was eyeing us both with disfavor. "Bombs are not toys, and accidents are often serious."

I looked at my right hand, imagining what someone would feel like to have most of their fingers blown away. They probably wouldn't feel a thing for a moment, except disbelief that part of them was gone, then the blood and the pain would come in an overwhelming wave. I repressed a shudder.

Joyce's steely voice intruded. "Dana, are you planning to take notes?"

"Oh yes, of course."

Joyce gave a tight smile to the rest of the class. "Now Dana has decided to listen, we'll go ahead with a list of common household chemicals that can be used in bomb-making."

I dutifully wrote down alcohol (drinks, solvents), acetone (nail polish remover, paint thinner), butane (cigarette lighter refills), ammonium hydroxide (household ammonia), ammonium nitrate (instant cold packs, fertilizer).

"That last item, ammonium nitrate in the form of fertilizer," said Joyce buoyantly, "was used in the Kansas City federal building bomb."

As she detailed with approval some of the blast

statistics from that outrage, I glanced around at my fellow students, then at Joyce. Monsters. They were monsters, every one of them. We all chatted and joked together, but I might as well have belonged to another species.

"Now, back to basics. A few words about Molotov cocktails." Joyce spoke of these street weapons with nostalgic affection. "I've used these beauties many times, and their very simplicity, a bottle and a rag, makes them wonderfully versatile. To make an effective, self-igniting firebomb I suggest kerosene and motor oil be mixed with a very flammable liquid such as petrol — gasoline to you, Fergus. Take care to shake well before lighting the wick."

She might have been giving instructions for taking cough medicine.

"More sophisticated Molotovs use a gelling agent that will stick to a wall or to the sides of a vehicle. An even more refined version has paper that has been soaked in a solution of potassium chlorate and sugar. When the paper dries, it's glued to the outside of the bottle. Deployed, this Molotov is guaranteed to work spectacularly well."

Joyce finished the session with a stern lecture on safety issues — no smoking, make sure there's good ventilation, wear a face shield or at the very least industrial goggles, use gloves when handling corrosive chemicals, and never, ever take a bomb for granted.

"Ever thrown a cocktail?" asked Cliff as we walked over to the main tent for afternoon refreshments.

"A martini several times," I said, "and once, I believe, a Harvey Wallbanger."

He sent me a pitying look. "I meant a Molotov."

"No," I said, "I've always been behind the scenes, but now I want to get involved. That's why I'm here."

"That's great," Cliff said, obviously applauding my choice to join the front line. "There's nothing like the rush you get when you're really *doing* something." His young, freckled face was earnest. "Like getting 'em down and kicking the shit out of them. It's the *best*."

"That's all right for you boys," I said, "but I'm more hands-off. I'd rather light a fuse."

The second session after lunch was the compulsory course Government Responses to Terrorism, and Siobhan was the instructor. I plunked myself right in front of the class, thinking that this was one time I'd love to be teacher's pet.

Siobhan was casually dressed in the standard khaki shorts and shirt, but she still presented a formal, somewhat forbidding persona. Her long hair was held by a comb in a loose twist, which should have looked casual but somehow seemed elegant.

She began crisply. "During the course we'll be studying different governments' strategies to contain terrorist threats, but today we'll look at the topic in general terms. The authorities generally strive to have the full complement of urban terrorism response teams in place within two hours of the terrorist action."

As she spoke she sketched a diagram on the whiteboard. "Unless there is intelligence to prove otherwise, the leaders of the response teams will assume that there are biological or chemical weapons, and possibly bombs, and have squads ready to deal with those particular threats. A perimeter defense will be set up immediately, and this will make it very difficult if not impossible for you to escape, so you leave the target area well before this point."

"What about suicide bombers, and the like?"

Siobhan grinned at Evonne. "You were planning that role?"

"Get off the grass! No way would I suicide." Evonne looked around at the class. "Not that I've got anything against them, mind — it's just not me."

"Well," said Siobhan dryly, "any suicide bomber will, as a job description, not be leaving the area. I trust that all of you, however, make an early escape, because the next step taken will flush you out if you haven't. This is a series of sector sweeps, where the teams are alert for mines, booby traps, sniper fire, and contamination of any sort."

She tapped the board with her marking pen. "Outside this perimeter other specialized bodies will be setting up command centers to cover medical needs and law enforcement. In addition, trained coordinators will be brought in to work with local, state, and federal agencies."

"So the idea is to have a multipronged attack," Rob suggested. "Booby-trapped biological would be good."

"Biological is good," said Siobhan, "because these weapons are especially frightening, and it is very important that the media and the public believe that there is a credible terrorist threat. Never underestimate the importance of PR, and be aware that encouraging distrust between the government and its citizens is advantageous. Hints that the public is not being told everything, that there is a conspiracy of some sort, can be extremely valuable."

As she went on to discuss in detail the psychological elements of a terrorist attack, I sat back to review my options. Tomorrow we would begin working in teams to prepare for the assassination assignment. I had to have concrete, accurate facts for ASIO, but I was sure team members would not be given full details about the strike. Edification was definitely into the need-to-know mind-set, and wisely so, as it was by far the best security measure to take. That meant I needed to cultivate one or more of the instructors, so that I'd have a source of reliable information.

Siobhan, being my official mentor, was my best bet, but I'd learned to examine all possibilities, so I considered the rest of the instructors, one by one.

Konrad? Of all of them, I found him the most formidable. Perhaps I was influenced by the overall impression of his broken nose, kung fu hands, and that disturbing snake tattoo. Somehow I couldn't see myself persuading him to spill the beans on anything.

Joyce was clearly not to be considered — if Aaron was right, she wished me harm, and even if he wasn't correct about this, I had no doubt that Joyce disliked me comprehensively.

Brit, however, could be the one to cultivate. We'd established a friendship of sorts, and if I worked at it, I was convinced Brit might come to think of me as someone to confide in, although she was no fool, and I would have to be careful not to play my part too broadly.

I frowned over Vince. Suddenly his attitude toward me had become quite pleasant, but I suspected there was some hidden agenda. Sex, maybe? Or, chilling thought, he was intending to play me along, because he or some of the others had suspicions about me.

Gary? Yes, a real possibility. And so was Aaron. They were the sort of guys that in other circumstances, I could have a drink and a laugh with — friends at a superficial level who talked too much when they were drunk. The fact that there was apparently no alcohol in the camp derailed that strategy, unfortunately.

My thoughts came back to Siobhan. She was answering a question from Wade, her clear English voice cool in the hot tent. I was sure I hadn't imagined the undercurrent in her words yesterday. A trickle of excitement ran down my spine. I admonished myself, *Work before pleasure*.

I had to smile. If I was very fortunate, perhaps the two would be combined.

At the close of the session I said to her, "Carry your books, ma'am?"

Siobhan gave me a considering look. "If you like."

There were only a couple of folders. I put them under one arm and gestured for her to lead the way. Naturally it was raining again, so we made a dash for the admin. tent, arriving damp and laughing.

"Where do you want them?" I asked, indicating the folders. I was suddenly aware that we were quite alone, and that the rain had become so hard that it was buffeting the tent with heavy blows.

"Over here."

I jumped at a crack of thunder, followed almost immediately by blue-white lightning.

"Are you frightened of thunderstorms?" she asked.

I handed her the folders. "No."

"I hate them."

She leaned forward, very slowly, and kissed me lightly on the lips. I felt an amazing shock, as though I'd been zapped by some extraordinary force.

Thunder crashed again. Involuntarily my arms went around her, and I kissed her back, but not lightly. It was a knee-weakening, heart-racing, I-want-you-now kiss. And she responded.

"Ah," I groaned, "we must have more than this."

Siobhan gave a low laugh. "I'm on guard duty tomorrow night," she said.

"A secret rendezvous? You think I'll sneak around for you?"

She smiled. "I'm hoping so."

CHAPTER SEVENTEEN

I was slowly building up a mental dossier for each person in the camp, drawing the material from casual conversations, overheard comments, chance remarks, my own oblique questions, and finally the impressions I'd picked up from day-to-day contact with everyone.

There might well be useful information on individuals in the filing cabinets I'd noticed in the admin. tent, but at this stage I wasn't willing to run the risk of being caught going through the files. It wouldn't hurt, though, to make an assessment of the situation, so after I'd had my morning shower, rinsed out my laundry, and hung the wet items on the clothesline strung under a camouflage net, I casually wandered in that direction.

As usual for this early hour, there was no one else around. I walked quickly, avoiding puddles and treading as lightly as possible past the row of instructors' tents. I knew one near the middle was Siobhan's because I'd observed her leaving it. My pace slowed as I grew level with her tent. I had no intention of opening the flap and saying, "Surprise! It's me!" but I couldn't help imagining her sleeping face, which led me to imagine the sleeping rest of her, which led me to —

"You're up early."

My heart gave a startled jump. I swung around to see Gary, who, hands jammed into the pockets of his shorts, was regarding me with a questioning smile.

"Sh." I gestured at the tents. "You'll wake everyone."

"Won't hurt them." Gary took my arm. "If you don't mind, I'll join your morning stroll. I need to stretch my legs."

I wanted to shake off his touch — the raw, peeling skin on his hands was suddenly repugnant, and his pale hair and coarse face disquieting.

"We had quite a discussion about you last night," he said, finally releasing me as we set off walking.

"Really?" I calmed my fluttering nerves with a deep breath. "Should I be worried?"

"Why would you say that?"

I turned an innocent face to him. "Why? I just assumed that it was something to do with Norbert."

"Your brother's disappeared into thin air, and the media have lost interest. And our discussion wasn't about him, although indirectly he was an issue."

We were heading out of the camp and toward the camouflaged four-wheel drives. I wanted to examine them closely, particularly to find out whether the ignition keys were left in the vehicles or kept somewhere else, but this was clearly not a project I could accomplish this morning.

"Isn't it beautiful, this time of day?" I said.

"Aren't you interested in why you were a topic of conversation?"

I shrugged my disdain. "If you're going to tell me, you will. If you're not, you won't."

"That's the spit-in-the-eye attitude I like. And that's why I nominated you for the lead role in your group."

I had a feeling this wasn't going to be something that would delight me. "The lead role?"

"You're a good shot."

I nodded agreement. Handguns weren't freely available in Australia or Britain, but Dana Wright had been a formidable opponent in competition with target pistols, which were available through registered gun clubs. And privately I thought I was probably a better shot than she was, and with a wider range of weapons.

Gary said, "I persuaded the others that you were the best bet, and they agreed that you're the one to take out the target if your team's selected."

"Hey," I said, "I'm flattered, but I don't get why you're so convinced I'm the one to do it."

"You've got what it takes, Dana. You won't panic

like the others might when the pressure's on, and you can think fast on your feet. Like I said, you're the best of your bunch."

"Who's the lead in the other group?" I asked.

Gary gave a short laugh. "Christ, can't you guess? Mokhtar — there wasn't any other choice. Nothing like a cold little psycho with a gun. He'll really enjoy the kill, I can tell."

"And I won't?"

Gary looked at me with real affection. "You'll do it well because it's your job," he said. "I like that."

We came to the camouflaged vehicles and stopped beside them. "Norbert will still be looking for me," I said. "I presume that's why he was mentioned in your discussions last night."

"Right on. And I pointed out that it was a non-issue." He startled me by reaching out and ruffling my hair. "Even so, I'm afraid you'll have to go from blond to brunet."

"But blondes have more fun. Everyone knows that."

Gary tilted his head and looked me over. "You know," he said reflectively, "having dark hair might really suit you."

I gave him a cheeky grin. "Would you take me more seriously?"

"Darl," he said, "I take you seriously enough right now."

I chatted to Rob over breakfast about nothing in particular, then Evonne joined us and the conversation turned nasty. "Bloody greenies," she said, slapping her plate and mug on the table and dropping her substantial weight onto the bench.

Rob put down his spoon. "What do you mean by that?"

Obviously in a foul mood, Evonne snarled, "What don't you understand? *Bloody* or *greenies*?"

Before Rob, whose pale face had gone an unflattering shade of puce, could respond, I broke in with, "Heavens, Evonne, what's got you so upset?"

She jabbed a thumb in Aaron's direction. "That fuck-wit Aaron was going on and on about the bloody environment. Makes me sick! We've got enough trouble with all the bloody Asians getting into the country, and all he wants to do is to hug bloody trees."

I saw that Rob had his lips compressed, obviously in an effort to restrain himself.

Evonne snapped a bite out of her toast, and chewing, narrowed her eyes at Rob. "You're one of them, I suppose."

"Dead right," said Rob. "And I happen to think trees are more important than people — especially people like *you*."

He settled back with the satisfied expression of one who has delivered a witty riposte.

Putting her hands on the edge of the table as if to leap to her feet, Evonne ground out, "You little shit. Don't you think I seen you sneaking around spying on everybody, then running to tell tales to Konrad?"

Rob did leap to his feet. Shoving his face close to hers, he said in a low growl, "You thick-necked bitch!"

I thought it was fortunate that at this point Rob made a gesture of contempt then immediately stalked off, because the reference to Evonne's neck had obviously struck home, and I was sure that if he had stayed for a full confrontation he would have suffered some sort of bodily harm.

Waiting until Evonne's stream of obscenities had dribbled to an occasional expletive, I said, "What in the world did you catch Rob doing? I mean, he's a bit of an odd guy, but I never thought of him as a sneak."

"A sneak?" said Evonne with heavy scorn. "He's a bloody plant, if you ask me."

"He's not!" I said with wide eyes. "A plant? You mean for Edification?"

"You got it."

I shook my head. "I reckon he fooled me." The look I sent Evonne was tinged with admiration. "How come you tumbled to him?"

Gratified, she said, "Had my eye on him. Those environmental types are always little shits." She looked at me sharply. "Are you —"

"An environmentalist? Hell, no. I believe in progress."

She grunted. "Okay, then."

"So tell me about Rob. I'm afraid that up to now I've been quite friendly with him."

This amused Evonne. "So I hear. Fergus practically had you shacked up together."

She demolished the rest of her toast, took a gulp of tea, then said, "You know how we were all searched in bloody Darwin? No cell phones, no cameras, no nothing? Well, yesterday I just happened to see Rob with something he wasn't supposed to have, one of those minirecorders you slip in your pocket. Voice-activated. Know what I'm talking about?"

"Uh-huh," I responded, rapidly running through my conversations with Rob. I couldn't think of anything I'd said that could blow my cover.

"So," said Evonne, warming to her story, "I knew he didn't know I'd twigged to him, so I watched him. All day he was super friendly, chatting with everyone, the little bastard. Then last night I saw him say something to Konrad, and slip out of the tent. A minute later Konrad followed."

She gave a snort of laughter. "Could have been a couple of poofters, I suppose, but I was betting not."

"And?"

With a pleased smile, she went on, "Never knew I was there. Rob gave Konrad the recorder, and Konrad handed him a replacement one." She lifted one corner of her mouth in an accomplished sneer. "Fucking Rob's a regular little spy, like I said. Get the picture?"

I got the picture.

We had our first team meeting after breakfast. Konrad and Gary set down team objectives to help us prepare exhaustively for the strike. We were to research the best way to travel incognito to and from the scene, plan the assassination down to the last second, and establish escape routes from the immediate area.

Konrad reminded us that the team not chosen for the kill would be involved in diversionary tactics so that it would appear to the authorities that there were two simultaneous terrorist attacks.

Since no one else had asked, I was forced to be the one to say, "Who's the target?"

"A man in the public eye, but not at the very top. This is an exercise, after all."

Patsy's nostrils flared. "Why go to all this trouble if we're not going to kill someone worthwhile?" she demanded.

"Oh, the guy's worthwhile, all right," said Gary. Ignoring Konrad's cautionary glare, he added, "Fancies himself the antiterrorism czar. We thought it unlikely that any of you would have an objection to offing him."

I knew instantly whom we were to kill. After several terrorist scares, the Australian government had appointed a committee headed by a newly retired police commissioner, Rex Leffing, to study and report on terrorist threats to the nation. That made Leffing the target.

"I've got a problem, Konrad," Fergus announced, his sandy eyebrows clenched in a frown. "What if one of us gets captured or wounded or even killed?"

"None of you will carry any identification. If any of you are wounded, we will make strenuous efforts to remove you from the scene."

"And captured?"

"No one will be captured," said Konrad. "I'm not implying for one moment this is a suicide mission, but there's no way Edification can allow the essential work we do to be compromised in any way."

To no one's surprise, Evonne immediately announced, "I've said it before, and I'll say it again — there's no way I'm killing myself."

"You won't have to," said Mokhtar coldly. "If the circumstances indicate it, I'm sure Edification will do it for you."

There was a pause while everyone looked to Konrad for a contradiction or comment. He remained impassive.

"Come on, people," said Gary. "The mission's going to go like clockwork, no worries."

When Gary went on to announce that, depending on the team chosen, I would be firing the fatal shot for Team Orange and Mokhtar for Team Yellow, there were a few rumbles of discontent. Cliff thought he, not Mokhtar, should lead Yellow, but Konrad soon shot that down with references to Cliff's relative inexperience.

Wade, who'd quite warmed to me before, scowled in my direction and complained that he'd already carried out a successful assassination, so he had experience on his side. "And what has Dana done, eh? So why her?"

When Gary detailed the minor part that Wade had played in the murder of the Malaysian politician, Wade subsided, grumbling unhappily.

While Konrad distributed a sheet headed in businesslike manner, *ESSENTIAL STEPS TO ACHIEVE OUR GOAL*, I glanced at my team members. Wade still looked miffed, but when I caught his eye and smiled, he gave me a nod of acknowledgment, a good sign. Evonne seemed quite content, although I had a suspicion the subject of suicide would come up again. Fergus wore a worried frown and was tapping nervously with his pen until Patsy leaned over and snatched it from him.

We broke up with Konrad promising that the hard

work would start the next day. In the meantime, we were to check in with our mentors before the next class began.

I obeyed this instruction with alacrity, finding Siobhan tapping away on a laptop in the admin. tent. Unhappily, Joyce and Brit were there too, and were shortly joined by their charges, Patsy and Rob.

Taking advantage of the hum of discussions going on with the others, I said in a low voice to Siobhan, "Evonne told me at breakfast that Rob was secretly recording conversations for Konrad."

I'd thought she might dissemble, but Siobhan just nodded calmly and said, "Yes, we do it every camp as a security measure. Rob wasn't a good choice — he shouldn't have been caught."

Well, so much for surprising her into some vital admission. "Okay," I said, "I'm here to be mentored."

We discussed elements of the team preparation for twenty minutes or so, then Joyce pointed out that the next class was about to start.

"See you later," said Siobhan.

Her smile held infinite promise.

I tried to concentrate in Gary's class Attacks on Urban Targets, but terrorist assaults on power, water, and airport facilities didn't have a fraction of the fascination the subject of Siobhan held for me at the moment.

I did pay close attention in the subsequent class, as it was Joyce's basic bomb-making, and I had no intention of losing my fingers, or indeed, any part of my anatomy. We concentrated on the ignition of bombs, becoming familiar with simple fuses, electric fuses, mercury switches, and tripwires. Joyce promised us that we would be taking a trek from the camp and actually exploding some devices tomorrow. Her face glowed as she said this, and I hoped it wasn't in anticipation of my imminent maiming.

I had the opportunity to study the object of my rising desire after the evening meal, when she taught Strategies to Panic the Public. I also had time to contemplate why I was so swamped with passion for someone who was essentially a stranger — and a terrorist. Perhaps, I reasoned, it was the phenomenon often observed to occur under the stress of war — sex as a fervent reaffirmation of life. Or perhaps I was having myself on, and all I was experiencing was healthy lust.

I listened to the class with wandering attention, although it was essentially interesting. Siobhan was pointing out that in the general public's case it is the fear of the attack that is most potent, and that there were a few words that could ignite unthinking terror. These words included *plutonium, anthrax,* and *bubonic plague*, especially if the last were called *Black Death*.

The actual deployment of more than a sample of these life-threatening items wasn't necessary. The general public wasn't informed, and ignorance led to panic. Disinformation, implications that the government was involved in a massive cover-up, selective leaks to the media — these were all useful strategies to convince citizens that their government was lying to them and that some dreadful threat was about to decimate the population.

The class ended, and while a couple of people went

to get a late cup of coffee or tea, most headed for the tents. I lingered until everyone had left. Siobhan said softly, "I'll come to your tent, but it'll be late."

Could one faint with desire? I might be about to find out. "It's a date," I said, a tremor in my voice.

CHAPTER EIGHTEEN

It was late — almost one-thirty. I was lying on my bed, still fully dressed. I'd planned to spend the time dozing in the darkness, but my mind and body were both wide awake. The tent next to mine was empty, but it wasn't much of a buffer. We would have to be very quiet. Even that thought was exciting.

"Dana?" came the whisper I'd been imagining for the last hour. I opened the flap of my tent, and she squeezed past me to sit on the end of my bed.

"You're here," I murmured, idiotically.

"I am," she agreed. "Do you have plans?"

"You're my mentor," I whispered, "so I'm duty bound to follow your instructions."

"And my desires?"

A flame ignited deep within me. I felt its glow could fill the tent. "Those too, I suppose."

"I desire you, right now, as fast as possible."

"There isn't much room."

"We'll improvise."

"If the camp bed gets broken," I said primly, "I'm not going to be responsible."

"Oh, I think you will be."

It was almost completely dark, although the faint silver of moonlight deflected through the mesh ventilation panels of the tent let me see that Siobhan, half reclining on my bed, was unbuttoning her shirt, sliding it off her shoulders, undoing her bra...

"Take off your clothes," she said, "and that's a mentor's order."

Although reckless to feel my bare skin against hers, I was well aware of the strictures of the little tent. "It'll take a little time, with both of us undressing," I observed. I meant to sound cool, but my voice was unsteady.

"Not too much time. Please."

It was the *please* that did it. I heard buttons pop as I ripped off my shirt. The boots I was wearing presented more of a challenge, but I overcame that too. "I've obeyed your order," I said. "Was there something else?"

"Improvise."

I kissed her neck, felt the heat radiating from her skin, said thickly, "We've got to be quiet. No cries of ecstasy."

Her laugh was breathless, yearning. "You're promising ecstasy? On our first date?"

My teeth found a nipple, and she gasped.

"Oh, God," I murmured against her breast. "I'm going to self-destruct."

"Don't do that. Let *me* destroy you."

My hands were under her, I felt her ribs through her burning skin, I slid down the length of her, lifted her to my mouth. And I was conqueror, her taste my reward, her bucking, frantic wildness my validation.

Then I was vanquished, submitting to the fire. The limitations of the cramped space, the darkness, the tent, the Kimberleys — all disappeared, supplanted by a howling vortex that sucked from me any sense of Dana, or Denise, or any identity at all. I had become pure, unfettered sensation.

I could not kiss her more deeply, open myself to her more completely, desire her touch more fiercely.

For one precious moment she and I were united beyond words, beyond grief or happiness.

Then reality began to trickle back. We were jammed together on the narrow bed, our laboring breaths mingling in the semidarkness. I hugged her tighter, willing the sense of otherness to stay, but it faded like a dream.

"The bed?" I said. "Did it survive?"

"Don't ask."

I smiled, too spent to laugh.

Siobhan broke our embrace and maneuvered until she was resting on one elbow and looking down at me.

I couldn't see her face distinctly, but her words were very clear.

"Who are you?" she said. "And don't say you're Dana Wright. You're not. I know that because I've met her."

It seemed to me the silence between us had gone on for a long time. I could hear her breathing, feel the jut of her hip against my side. The darkness in the tent hadn't changed, but I felt as though a brilliant flash had gone off in my eyes.

At last I said, "I'm Dana Wright."

"Who are you with? The DIO?"

Australia's top-secret Defence Intelligence Organization was so covert that we in ASIO hardly knew what they were doing, and the general public had no idea. "I don't know what you mean," I said.

"ASIO? Or have you been coopted by MI6? The CIA?"

"I don't understand."

"Dana —" She broke off to laugh ruefully. "That's the name I have to use, unless you care to tell me your own."

"What's *your* real name?"

I didn't expect her to reply, but she said, "My middle name's Siobhan. My first is Mary."

Mary? She didn't look like a Mary. She didn't feel like a Mary. "I'd stick to Siobhan," I said.

There was urgency in her low voice as she leaned forward to say, "Please. I need to know who you're with. It's vital."

When I didn't answer her, Siobhan let out her breath in a long sigh. "Have you heard of the Hurdstone Peace Foundation?"

Here was something I could admit to freely, so I said, "Of course."

The Hurdstone Peace Foundation had been created with Ash Hurdstone's millions in the eighties, and as his wealth in British electronics grew, so did his investment in the foundation that bore his name. With a head office in Switzerland, and dedicated to the promotion of peace throughout the world, the Foundation had planted workers in corrupt companies, had infiltrated many terrorist groups, and had worked tirelessly to overthrow totalitarian governments. Hurdstone employees had to be entirely dedicated to the Foundation's premise, as many of them would go undercover for years, in the process getting deeply entrenched in the organizations they were attacking from within.

ASIO, the CIA, and similar national security services did not support Ash Hurdstone or the activities he promoted, but this was not because the Foundation didn't have laudable objectives which it very often achieved. It was true that Hurdstone disregarded both local and international laws when it suited him and had yet to pay for such transgressions in any meaningful way. More embarrassing to government bodies in different countries was the fact that the Hurdstone Peace Foundation very often succeeded where they failed.

In the United States, for example, Hurdstone had published on the Foundation's Web site the names, descriptions, and photographs of white supremacists who were well advanced in a scheme to attack the

Supreme Court when it was next in session. Not only had the information been entirely accurate, the FBI and CIA had not been aware of the scope or intention of the attack, and had to scramble to cover their backs when influential politicians began to ask uncomfortable questions.

If Siobhan was a Hurdstone counterterrorist plant, then she had been working for three years to white-ant Edification from within. Or she was lying, and this was a bizarre test for Dana Wright to pass or fail.

"Have you met Ash Hurdstone?" I asked, expecting a negative reply, as the now billionaire many times over was a recluse, and had not been seen in public for many years.

"I've met him. Many times."

I persisted. "Recently? There are rumors that he died."

"Ash Hurdstone isn't dead," said Siobhan. "I should know. He's my father."

CHAPTER NINETEEN

In the morning the images of the night had the surreal hyper-reality of a dream. We'd talked on for half an hour before she left. I hadn't admitted my true identity, but had continued without heat to insist that I was Dana Wright. I'd questioned Siobhan closely about the Hurdstone Peace Foundation, and she'd come through with flying colors.

Siobhan, Ash Hurdstone's daughter? It wasn't impossible. But was it probable?

I'd asked her one last question as she'd struggled

in the confined space to get dressed. "The assassination — are you intending to do anything to prevent it?"

She'd been fumbling with the laces of her boots when I asked this, and had suddenly become quite still. "The short answer is yes, but the tricky thing is to find a way to do it without making anyone suspicious of me. I think you may be the solution to that problem."

I would have gone on to ask how, but Siobhan had pointed out, quite accurately, that we were both exhausted, and should talk later when we'd make more sense.

She'd paused, kneeling at the tent's flap, and said, "Think on this, Dana. I've taken a chance and told you who I am. Won't you trust me too?"

I'd thought I'd be awake all night, but after Siobhan left I checked the bed — she'd been joking, it wasn't broken — and then had fallen in a deep, dreamless sleep.

In the clear light of morning I realized that if she were a Hurdstone plant, and his daughter, then she'd have backup somewhere close. Of that I was absolutely sure. Siobhan had been a trusted member of Edification for three years, and had helped set up Camp E, so she knew the area, as well as being fully informed about Edification's security measures. What had been impossible for ASIO was very possible for her. If I saw her backup with my own eyes, then I'd be inclined to believe she was telling me the truth.

Siobhan came in late to breakfast. She looked drawn, almost gaunt, and even her burnished hair seemed dulled by fatigue. I thought for some reason she'd ignore me, but she came straight over to the table where I sat with Patsy and Cliff, and said, "After your team meeting there's a mentoring session for everyone. Dana, I'm not happy with your grasp of some of the details we discussed yesterday, so I want you to be prepared, if necessary, to work well into your meal break tonight."

I thought it appropriate to protest, so I moaned, "Fair go, I do enough as it is."

Siobhan's implacable expression didn't change. "We have high standards here."

I drooped a little. "Okay."

After she'd walked off to join the breakfast queue, Cliff said sympathetically, "Jeez, that's a bit much."

"Hard taskmaster," added Patsy, sending Siobhan a cold glance. "It gets some of them like that — the power I mean. Specially the women. You should go to Konrad and complain."

"Siobhan just wants Team Orange to do well."

My mention of the team triggered a bitter snarl from Patsy. "I've already asked for a transfer from Yellow to Orange, but nothing's doing. I absolutely cannot stand that little prick." This time her laser stare was directed in Mokhtar's direction. "You'd think he was the only person in the world who could carry out an efficient assassination."

The incongruity of Patsy's remark made me grin, but I sobered quickly when I pondered the imminent attack on Rex Leffing. If I was only sure that Siobhan was telling the truth, then I might have a way to get an urgent message to the outside world.

* * * * *

"Make it snappy," said Joyce, her face squinched into a sour-lemon expression. "Bloody hell! You'd be the most hopeless class I've ever had."

Her bomb class, me included, straggled along the trail, sweat pouring from our faces. The clouds had parted and the sun beat down, sucking every bit of moisture possible into the air. The humidity had to be close to a hundred percent. It was like wading in hot water.

Each of us was laden with bomb-making items. I hadn't asked what was in my canvas backpack Joyce handed me, but being paranoid, I'd swapped it with one that someone else had put down for a moment.

Joyce had marshaled us in a line and told us we were going down into a gorge that would contain the noise of the explosions when we detonated our bombs. She'd led off at a good pace, and we had hurried after her.

Now we were on the difficult part of the trail, where it zigzagged down a steep drop. In parts the only way to be safe was to look for secure hand grips and move with care. Insects zinged around our faces, and Rob in particular kept swiping ineffectually at them.

I noticed Evonne, for all her square heaviness, was moving smoothly, as was Fergus. Patsy was having trouble, and eventually Fergus took her pack. This was not out of a sudden sense of chivalry on his part, but because Joyce bellowed, "For God's sake, Fergus, take Patsy's pack before she goes arse over tit all the way to the bottom!"

The bushland was gorgeous. Trees clung to the incline, their twisted roots delving into every cranny.

There was a sound of water splashing, birds called overhead, shy wildflowers hid in crevices, the lacy fronds of ferns trembled in the breeze that swept up the rockface.

To give Patsy time to recover, we all rested for a moment. Evonne, realizing that she had stopped next to a large branch on which a goanna rested, shrieked. When the huge lizard, understandably alarmed, opened its mouth wide at this, Evonne shrieked once more.

"Shut up," yelled Joyce, whose patience was clearly wearing thin. Various unkind suggestions were made as to what Evonne should do to cope with wildlife, then we started off again.

The descent was well worth it when we reached the unspoiled views at the bottom. The gorge was actually a waterway that was open, Joyce said, to the sea, but this was hidden from us by a sharp bend in the channel. The deep, green water eddied as the tide turned. On the other side the sandstone cliff fell sheer, but where we were there was a wide shelf of mostly smooth rock, dotted with the remains of boulders that had fallen from the heights above us. Many had smashed into pieces, but there were some monster rocks that had remained whole.

I looked up to where a sea eagle soared, its wings extended. Below a small flock of black-and-white pelicans floated serenely on the water.

"That's where some of you will board a boat when you leave for the strike," said Joyce, pointing to one huge slab of rock at the edge of the water that by chance had formed a natural jetty.

She directed us to put our packs in the shade of

one of the fallen behemoths. "Don't go anywhere near the water," she instructed.

"Why not?" Cliff belonged to those people who always wanted to do whatever it was they were told not to.

"All right — *go*," said Joyce. "Crocs aren't choosy."

From their faces everybody was recalling the description of a saltwater crocodile's deadly penchant for lurking in murky water, and its technique for dispatching its dinner-to-be. Cliff didn't go near the water.

By the end of an hour and a half of smoke bombs, pipe bombs, rocket bombs, and compressed-gas bombs, I was heartily sick of explosions, especially as I had been on full alert for the whole time, just in case Joyce tossed me a grenade, or set off a radio-controlled device when I was nearby. My caution was wasted. Joyce appeared to have no interest in me, concentrating instead on detonations, a pastime she obviously found rewarding.

Although Joyce seemed reluctant to end our session, hunger prevailed, so we gathered everything together in somewhat lighter backpacks and clumped together at the base of the cliff.

Patsy, appalled, asked if we had to climb the path we'd descended earlier. "Well, of course," said Joyce. "If there was an easier way, we'd have come down it, wouldn't we?"

I'd always found it much harder to go down than up as far as a steep path was concerned, and today wasn't an exception. Soaked with sweat, we all made it to the top in a shorter time than we'd taken to descend, although Patsy, scarlet-faced and wheezing, had to be given a boost at every difficult section. We were observed in our efforts by a flock of brilliantly colored lorikeets who screeched amused comments to each other about our progress.

Striding along the track to the camp, I thought longingly of a cold shower, but we only just made it back in time for lunch, so all of us, gritty, tired, and hot, dumped our backpacks with Joyce and went into the dining tent.

Next was another class with Vince on kidnapping skills, then after a mid-afternoon break, the team groups, followed by meetings with our individual mentors. The athletic sex, the lack of sleep, and the tension I was feeling all combined to make the rest of the afternoon float by at one remove.

Collecting my energy, I slogged over to the admin. tent to meet up with Siobhan. The sun had disappeared, and the cloud cover hung low and sullen.

"It's too hot in here," Siobhan said, grabbing two chairs. "Let's sit outside and hope for a breeze."

Others were trying the same strategy, but we positioned ourselves under a tall gum tree out of earshot of any of the other pairs and in a position where we could see anyone approach.

I looked around, thinking how exposed we were. "I'm worried someone can hear us. Has anyone a directional microphone or any other listening device?"

"There are bugs in the main tent and in the classrooms. They're not worried about anything out here."

I felt a wave of indignation. "They're bugging us? Bastards!"

She gave a full-throated laugh. "You're definitely one of a kind, Dana."

"And last night? Was I one of a kind then? Or just an easy lay?" I heard the bitterness in my own voice and was embarrassed by it.

Her face softened. "Last night was . . . unique. Exciting. I can't wait to do it again."

My vulnerability to this woman angered me. "That isn't what is important now."

My hostility blanked her face. She sat back, watching me.

"Have you got a backup?" I said. "Someone close whom you can contact?"

"Of course. He's camping quite close to here. His cover is that he's a naturalist, studying tropical centipedes."

"How do you contact him?"

"Not by spoken communication. I send him an electronic signal, he picks it up on a receiver, and we meet at a previously agreed time and place."

"I want to meet him."

She didn't hesitate. "All right, after the last session tonight. As soon as it finishes, go to the storage shed behind the kitchen tent."

"Don't tell me to be careful — I will be."

Siobhan leaned forward, her expression intense. "Dana, you can't know the full extent of Edification. It's taken me three years to really understand it. Edification is much more complex than you realize. It's like an iceberg, with most of the organization hidden under the surface. That's why I'm telling you the Leffing assassination should go ahead as planned — it's regarded as an important step in publicizing Edification to potential clients and increasing the organization's clout in terrorist circles. Several tiers of the Edification hierarchy will be in Sydney to see the action."

"This could just be a fantastic story you're spinning."

For the first time Siobhan looked defeated. "It could be."

I felt restless, trapped, angry, but with an effort I forced myself to be still, calm, reasonable. If Siobhan was who she said she was, then she walked in danger every moment of the day.

"There's something else," she said, her expression troubled. "I believe Norbert Cummins is getting closer to you."

Noticing that she didn't refer to him as my brother, I said, "Give me the bad news."

"A young man in Sydney, Howie Bradley, has been murdered. Beaten to death."

"Howie? In the Annandale TrekTrak office?" A picture of him rose in my mind, a girlie magazine in his hand, his prominent Adam's apple bobbing in his throat. "You think Norbert had something to do with it?"

"Yes, I do, but Konrad isn't so sure, and the others don't care. I happen to believe that Howie was keeping tabs on things, thinking that TrekTrak was some sort of shady deal. He collected any information he could because he was betting there was an angle that could make him money."

I visualized Howie sitting at the desk, his face vacant, all his attention apparently on the naked females in his magazine. But of course he could have been listening to every word Brit and I had said to each other.

We both looked up as Konrad approached. "Excuse me for interrupting, but I need to speak with you, Siobhan. Sorry, Dana."

"Hey, I welcome a break," I said cheerfully. "This is so all so intense."

I told myself I was meditating, but actually I half dozed for the fifteen minutes she was away. Smothering a yawn, I straightened on the uncomfortable metal chair as she returned. "Anything world-shattering?"

"I'm afraid so. The date of the strike has been moved up to the end of next week."

"Next week? That's not enough time to prepare."

"The original schedule had the Lord Mayor of Sydney presenting Leffing with the Lightner Humanitarian Award three weeks from now in a ceremony at the Sydney Town Hall. That's been changed because Leffing's a delegate at a conference on world terrorism being held in Geneva. It's going to be a rush, but Konrad says Edification's going ahead with the strike as a symbolic move against the world conference."

She touched my hand. Electricity zapped up my arm. "And Team Orange will be the one to carry out the strike. This means, of course, that you are the person firing the fatal shot."

"Good," I said, and meant it. If the assassination went ahead I would have some control over what happened.

* * * * *

The moon was riding a cloudy sky when I strolled in the direction of the storage shed. A few sprinkles of rain had fallen, so most people were still inside the main tent or hurrying off to complete preparations for bed. I gave the kitchen tent a wide berth and slipped through the trees toward the faint outline of the shed.

"Here," breathed Siobhan. She pulled me behind the little iron building. "This is Jeff."

"Hi," said the bulky shadow beside her. "Follow me."

We went deep into the bush, Jeff treading confidently as though it were bright daylight, with me behind him and Siobhan bringing up the rear. When we were some distance from the camp, he stopped. "Get behind this tree trunk, Dana. I want you to be able to recognize me when you see me again."

He had an English accent, more attenuated than Siobhan's, but pleasant. His flashlight illuminated a broad, strongly featured face, with heavy brows and a wide, humorous mouth. "Now let's see you." As I blinked in the light, he said, "You're close to Dana Wright, but you're not her."

"Don't tell me you claim to be her second-best friend. Is that it?"

He had a nice laugh. "Hardly. I knew her parents, and I met her a couple of times in London."

Siobhan took my hand, linking her fingers with mine. *Oh, hell*, I thought, *this is too elaborate to be a trap. If Konrad and company suspected me, then Vince would be bashing me right now.*

"My name's Denise," I said. "Denise Cleever. I work for ASIO."

CHAPTER TWENTY

"Denise?" said Siobhan. "I think I prefer Dana."

Jeff was all business. "We haven't much time. You can't be gone for too long. We need to plan, fast."

I said, "The strike doesn't have to go through. Arrests can happen as everyone leaves this area. Between us, Siobhan and I can provide enough evidence for convictions."

"That can't happen." Siobhan's low voice was urgent. "Everything that my father and the Foundation has done to destroy Edification will be wasted if you arrest only those who are associated with this camp. I told you, there's a huge secret structure, and those hidden leaders have to be drawn into the open. The Hurdstone Foundation is ready to share everything we know, as long as it means Edification is annihilated."

"You're willing to share *everything* with Australian security services?" This type of cooperation was not the Hurdstone Foundation's usual method of doing things.

"My father has agreed that it's my decision, and I say, under these urgent circumstances, we share everything."

I was too far in to turn back now. If Siobhan was about to betray me, then it was too late to do anything about it. I said to Jeff, "I'll give you a telephone number and the dialing sequences you must use. Eventually you'll speak to Livia. You'll need two code phrases."

Siobhan laughed when I gave them to him. "Tinkling Octupi?" she said. "And Rogue Ambiguity? You came up with both of them, didn't you?"

"How could you tell?"

"Seemed to have your touch."

Jeff and Siobhan conferred for a few moments about logistics, then Jeff said good-bye to me and slipped away silently into the darkness.

"We should go back separately," Siobhan said, holding my hand again. "We have to be very careful. Everything's on high alert. Konrad and the others have a lot at stake because it's vital that this exercise is successful."

We kissed slowly, drawing the moment out, then parted, making no plans to make love again. Walking back to the camp I felt a sudden surge of determination. If Siobhan had been willing to sacrifice three years of her life to bring Edification down, I was going to do my part to make sure that goal was attained.

The next days were tough. One positive thing was that Joyce's animosity toward me had obviously been put on hold while everyone concentrated on the Leffing strike. Mokhtar had been predictably furious when he found that Team Orange was the chosen one. It wasn't enough that his Team Yellow was to create a diversionary mock attack at Sydney airport using small explosive devices that would create more noise and smoke than any serious damage. Mokhtar wanted to kill.

It was a comfort to me to imagine him under arrest.

Gary had taken the lead in the preparation for the mission, rehearsing us unmercifully. "Go for the head, Dana," he'd yell. "We want this target dead, not wounded."

A head shot was much harder to achieve, and I practiced for hours with the weapon Edification wanted me to use — a sleek little Smith & Wesson Scandium Series revolver. It held only five rounds, but as Gary pointed out, I shouldn't need more than one if I did my job correctly.

It wasn't the weapon I would have chosen. I'd have preferred my subcompact Glock any day, but I was stuck with it and the intrinsic problem all little short-barreled guns had — lack of accuracy. And it was fitted with a suppressor, popularly called a silencer, and I'd never used one before. Nevertheless, I became quite proud of my marksmanship, and Gary was delighted with me.

As a team, we studied the area of the strike in great detail, poring over maps and street directories, and tracing various escape routes. The venue was excellent for an assassination, as the Sydney Town Hall, a grandly ornate Victorian building with a clock tower, sat in one of the busiest parts of the city. There were many streets available for escape, plus an underground railway station. Nearby were office buildings and department stores, and one entire city block adjacent to the Town Hall was taken up by the Queen Victoria Building, which was full of shops and restaurants and had myriad ways to enter and leave the structure.

Because of the compressed time frame, the travel arrangements for the strike were taken over by Brit and Vince. In order to be inconspicuous, and to prevent a potential witness associating us with a large group, we were split into pairs, each to leave the area by a different route under the care of an instructor.

I was paired with Wade — here was a true advantage to have him so generic in appearance — and we were under Konrad's care. I'd hoped for Siobhan, but perhaps it was better if we were not seen together too much.

Konrad, Wade, and I were to leave by sea in a fishing boat, travel around the coast to Derby, then fly out. The others would be retracing the route we'd taken from Kununurra, or picking up the Ibis Aerial Highway at the nearest light aircraft strip, or driving the long road to Broome.

I had very little chance to see Siobhan in private. Security had been stepped up, and now there were patrols all night. We stole a few moments together, but the risk to the plans to destroy Edification made these meetings full of anxiety. And I was terribly concerned about her safety. She'd had several meetings with Jeff during daylight hours because of the increased security at night, and had told me that they'd nearly been caught together by Vince, who had been given the added responsibility of keeping the perimeter of the camp secure during the day.

Our measurements had been taken, and suitable clothes were brought in for each of us in the roles were to play. The day before we were to depart for Sydney, Brit dyed my blond hair a rich, dark brown. The effect was quite shocking to me when I looked into the mirror she offered to me and saw my familiar face framed with dark hair. "What do you think?" I said.

Brit peered at me closely, as though I might be some alien who had dropped in. "Not bad." She ran her hand over her own impeccable hair. "Think you're better as a blonde. I mean, it's more lighthearted, if you see what I mean."

Then, before the evening meal, Gary called me into the admin. tent. All the instructors were present, and they examined my brunet self with interest. Vince even made, for him, a quite complimentary remark. I had decided that it *was* my charm that had won him over. Or maybe it was the fact that I made him laugh when he taught the grim subject of kidnapping.

"About the strike," said Gary without wasting time on pleasantries, "Konrad's got a couple of things to tell you."

I obediently looked at Konrad. His face emotionless, he said, "I don't need to impress on you how vital it is that this strike be successful. It's critical both for you and for Edification. Your weapon has five shots. Gary assures me you'll only need one, or two at the most."

He looked around at the other instructors, then went on, "We've all agreed that if any of your team is wounded, or about to be captured, and you're close enough, you're to take them out. Kill them."

I forced a smile. "And what about me? In that situation do I contemplate suicide?"

"That would be too much to ask, so . . ." Konrad jerked his head in Gary's direction.

Gary grinned. "Sorry, darl. Trust me, killing you will be last-resort stuff, I promise."

CHAPTER TWENTY-ONE

It's a brisk autumn day in Sydney, with a chill wind blunting the heat of the sunshine. I know there are ASIO agents and federal cops salted throughout the crowd that's gathered outside the overdecorated sandstone glory of the Sydney Town Hall.

If I turn my head to the left I should be able to locate Evonne and Wade, waiting to follow their script. They both have loud voices, and that's what will be needed.

For a moment a man near me looks like Norbert,

and my stomach clenches, but he moves his head and I can see it's a perfect stranger. I scan the crowd, but logic has made me relax. Even if Norbert is here, he won't recognize me because he's looking for the real Dana Wright.

I look behind me and spot Jeff. He's standing behind the knot of media people waiting at the bottom of the entrance steps to the Town Hall, and he gives me an almost imperceptible nod. I know he intends to reassure me, but when I get the chance — *if* I get the chance — I'll tell him he took a stupid risk doing that.

Gary, looking relaxed, is over to my right. He's ready to clear the way for us as we leave, or if he believes it necessary, to execute me.

Fergus is beside me, a TV camera balanced on his shoulder. He's wearing gloves. I expect him to say something, but he stares fixedly up the steps. I wait, notebook in one hand, microphone in the other, just one of the crowd of media waiting for something to happen.

I'm a little different, though. I'm wearing a flesh-colored glove on my right hand, and a revolver nestles in my pocket holster, so there is no betraying outline in the clean lines of my jacket. I'm wearing a navy suit, nice but not striking. I have on large-lens dark glasses, and my newly brown hair is center-parted in a style I never use.

There's a movement at the top of the steps. "Out of the way, mate," Fergus says, pushing forward. The reporter, his attention on the action above, ignores him.

Official guests are gathering, their smiles already

flashing for the television cameras. Rex Leffing, not smiling, appears in the center, the lord mayor by his side. The mayor, in full regalia, is talking animatedly. I have a fleeting, semihysterical thought that I might shoot him by mistake.

We media people press on up the steps. I'm closer, closer. I put my notebook in my left pocket, slip my gloved fingers around the gun. The revolver was originally silver, but it's been painted matte black so it won't reflect in the sunlight.

"Aim for his head," I've been commanded. I aim for Leffing's heart. The gun kicks in my gloved hand. The sound is a sibilant *phut*. Leffing looks surprised — even with the state-of-the-art protective vest he's wearing, the kick of the bullet will bruise him badly.

He goes down. Someone screams. Leffing's bodyguard has drawn his gun, but I know he won't shoot.

On schedule, Evonne shrieks — I have to admit she's good at it — and points off to the side as Wade shouts, "Stop him! He's getting away! He's got a gun!"

People crane to see, while those in the imaginary path of the gunman scramble to get clear.

Right now there should be the same confusion at Sydney International Airport, where, under Joyce and Siobhan's supervision, Team Yellow has filled the passenger terminal with smoke and the noise of explosions.

I've already returned the gun to its holster. Fergus lays the TV camera down on the steps, and we move quickly toward Gary. Wade and Evonne have already disappeared into the crowd, and are making a wide circuit around the building to get to the two waiting taxis — fakes, of course. Konrad will be sitting in one of them, waiting to hear our report.

"I said head shot," snarls Gary.

"I'm sorry," I say. "But I killed him, anyway."

CHAPTER TWENTY-TWO

When we'd all rendezvoused in Sydney before the strike the safe house had been in the suburb of West Ryde. It had been a rather shabby, unpretentious dwelling with a neglected garden and cheap furniture. There we'd all run through our roles yet again, and after pizza and beer, slept three to a room until an early fast-food breakfast brought to us from the closest McDonald's.

I'd met three more Edification people at the West Ryde house, Irene, John, and Randall, and had automatically memorized everything useful that might help identify them later. I knew this wasn't really necessary, as Siobhan had given Jeff details of our travel plans to pass on to Livia, so ASIO would have had us under intense surveillance since we'd left the Kimberleys.

I was interested in the relative power positions of our instructors and the three new Edification members. Vince and Aaron had stayed at Camp E, so that meant five instructors were in Sydney — Konrad, Joyce, Brit, Gary, and Siobhan.

Irene and John were clearly higher in the pecking order than Brit, Gary, and Siobhan, but Konrad and Joyce had a superior position. Randall was the junior in the group.

It soon became clear that Konrad had the most to lose if anything went wrong with the assassination. It was referred to several times as "Konrad's strike," and his concern that everything run without a hitch had been obvious.

Now, in the postassassination phase, Konrad was cautiously optimistic. As a driver took us across the Sydney Harbour Bridge in the bogus taxi, Konrad turned around in the front passenger seat to say, "A successful strike, I think."

"It was the best," said Fergus, who had hardly stopped talking since we'd entered the taxi. "We just stood around waiting for ages, and then Leffing came out and —"

"Dana, what's your evaluation?" interrupted Konrad.

"No probs. It went smoothly."

Gary was still irate. "Dana went for the body, not the head."

I spread my hands apologetically. "I couldn't get a clean shot at Leffing's head. Got him square in the chest, though."

Konrad allowed his anxiety to show. "You think he's dead, though, don't you?"

I shrugged. "If not, he soon will be."

In the back streets of Waverton we changed vehicles, leaving the revolver with the phony taxi driver. Gary drove us to Roseville, where we switched to another anonymous car. In both vehicles the radio was blaring the news that Leffing had been shot and had been rushed to the nearest hospital, but his present condition wasn't known.

We didn't return to the West Ryde place, but went to a second safe house in the upmarket suburb of Mosman. It was a step up from the other one, being a mansion with impressive iron gates and a panoramic view of Sydney Harbour.

Brit met us at the door. She patted my shoulder, smiling broadly. "Great stuff, Dana!"

With her was a man who radiated authority. He had prematurely white hair, a deeply tanned, brutal face, and a cultivated voice. He introduced himself as Larry and ushered us inside.

"What's the latest news?" Konrad asked as soon as the door closed behind us.

"Leffing's condition has just been given as grave. But he's not dead."

Konrad's wide mouth tightened at Larry's implied criticism. He turned to send a cold glance at me.

"Hey, guys," I said. "I guarantee he'll die. Trust me on that." I could say this with assurance, knowing ASIO's scenario for the situation.

Larry looked surprised to be addressed so casually. "I admire your confidence, Dana," he said in a dry tone.

The others had arrived, and were sitting watching television reports in the sumptuous living room. I took care not to look in Siobhan's direction. At this vital stage there must be nothing to suggest we were anything but instructor and student.

Mokhtar sneered when he saw me. "You botched it," he declared. "*I* would have killed Leffing outright."

"How did your smoke bombs at the airport go?" I inquired, deliberately reminding him of his secondary role.

Mokhtar scowled. Patsy, who had commandeered a dish of nuts from somewhere and was happily munching her way through them, said, "It was great. Lots of screams and shouts and people running around."

Cliff had the remote and was switching from channel to channel. It was apparent the assassination attempt had preempted most programs, as a progression of serious-faced newsreaders flicked across the screen.

"Give me that!" Evonne snatched the remote from Cliff. "You're just like my bloody son — can't stick on anything for more than a few secs."

She selected a channel. "I like this guy," she announced as an avuncular news anchor appeared on the screen. Evonne's timing was excellent. He was saying, his fleshy face arranged in somber lines, "We have breaking news. Ex-commissioner Rex Leffing, who had just received a humanitarian award, has died of grave wounds sustained in an attack at the Sydney Town Hall this afternoon."

Someone actually clapped. Konrad said, "Thank God!"

Larry, smiling, shook his hand. "That's more like it," he said. "How about champagne for everyone, eh?"

While I joined in the celebrations, I had a picture of Leffing wincing as the doctors examined his bruised chest. He'd be spirited away to be kept under wraps until all possible Edification members had been identified.

The West Ryde safe house would already be under the most intense covert surveillance, with telephones tapped, directional microphones pointed at windows, and all vehicles parked near the place tagged with tiny transmitters. Everyone entering the house would be photographed. Those leaving would be followed, and anyone they contacted would fall into the investigative net.

As soon as possible, similar surveillance would be directed at this Mosman house and its occupants.

As there must be nothing to alert the Edification hierarchy that ASIO and other security bodies were gathering information to destroy the organization, everything had to appear normal. This meant that Siobhan and I would both continue to play our roles and that the camp in the Kimberleys would be left undisturbed.

Konrad had decided that the return to the Kimberleys would be staggered, with he, Wade, and I leaving first, so that same day the three of us flew out of Sydney to retrace our route.

I tried to relax during the trip, but tendrils of uneasiness brushed across my mind. There were so many things that could go wrong, particularly with the number of agents, both here and overseas, who were involved in the investigations.

When I saw the *Sea Vagabond* waiting for us at Derby, I decided to forget my worries and enjoy the last leg of our journey. Spending too much time in close proximity to Konrad had frazzled my nerves, especially when he had insisted on sitting beside me in the series of flights we had taken to get to Derby.

Nor was Wade an ideal travel companion, as conversation with him for any length of time established that he was an unbelievably boring individual. I'd tried the trick of entertaining myself by investigating why I found him so wearisome, but had so bored myself that I'd dropped that activity fast.

Soon the soothing vistas of ocean and sky calmed me. Our boat kept reasonably close to the shore, passing countless bays and inlets, wild places where only birds and animals ruled. Cliffs fell to the tame sea, which licked the shore with docile waves. Now and then we saw a yacht or cabin cruiser, but most of the time it was as if we were the only humans in the world, skirting a primeval land.

I spent some time chatting to the captain, Lyle. He was an old guy, salt to the core, who'd lived his life on the ocean and confided that he found his time on dry land unsettling. He was well read, and we discussed Conrad and *Heart of Darkness* for a while. I turned the conversation to the subject of Konrad, who was sitting in the bow with Wade watching dolphins racing our vessel, leaping and diving with a silver skill that made me long to be in the water with them.

Lyle told me he'd done a lot of work for Konrad, mainly picking up people from Derby and Broome, and dropping them off near the Mitchell River National

Park. He laughed as he said, "These ecotour things he runs — what a joke! Soft quiche-eaters trying to rough it in the great outdoors."

He made haste to pat my hand, saying, "I don't mean you, love. You're not one of them. I can see you're fit and ready for anything." He inclined his head in Konrad's direction. "Got a thing going with him, have you?"

Erk! I resisted the impulse to clutch at my throat and make gurgling noises. Instead I said brightly, "Not with Konrad. There's someone else."

A stab of guilt startled me. How many someone-elses did I have? All the time I'd believed Siobhan was a terrorist, at some level I'd been able to rationalize that whatever I did with her was part of my job, and that Roanna, if she ever knew about it, would understand. But now . . .

"Someone else?" Lyle made a face at me. "That was the situation with my wife. Ran off with a scuba diver." His threw back his head and guffawed. "I never let her know it, but it was a great relief to me, I can tell you."

The trip took hours, but I was happy to doze on one of the bunks, or sit alone and watch the scenery unwind. Konrad hardly spoke to me, and Wade slept most of the time.

Lyle gave us a huge thermos of strong coffee and sandwiches, and I sat munching the thick brown bread and sharp cheese and thinking it was more delicious food than any four-star restaurant could provide.

Eventually we approached our destination. I couldn't see how Lyle could tell that any opening was there in the cliffs, but he turned starboard with utter confidence, threaded his way through sunken rocks and reefs, and slid the *Sea Vagabond* through the narrow entrance to the gorge. Seabirds rose in clouds as the sound of the motor echoed off the stone walls.

It was a magnificent place, I thought, my head flung back to look up at the rim of the cliffs far above. Wild and green and untouched by the grubby hands of tourists who left trails of debris behind them as they clicked cameras to capture trophy moments to display.

Well, not entirely untouched. We came slowly around the bend in the gorge and nudged up to the rock-slab jetty. The shelf was littered with the remains of bombs that we'd exploded in Joyce's lesson. From the water the perspective was quite different. The huge fallen boulders loomed larger, the cliff where the path was located seemed much more sheer.

Lyle helped us unload our things — we only had backpacks — shook hands with each of us, and, with a wave, edged the cruiser away from the stone jetty. He blasted his foghorn once as he disappeared around the bend, the bass sound echoing and reechoing from rocky wall to rocky wall.

"Well," said Konrad, hands on hips as he surveyed the scene, "we'd better get started."

We had taken only a few steps when a man came from behind one of the largest boulders. The double-barreled shotgun he held pointed unwaveringly at us.

"I've been waiting for you," he said in a clear, clipped English voice.

It was Norbert Cummins.

CHAPTER TWENTY-THREE

Norbert hadn't done much to change his appearance. His hair was cut shorter and he had the beginnings of a mustache, but he still looked the handsome, self-assured man that I had studied in photographs. Compared to us in our wrinkled khakis, Norbert looked impossibly dapper. He wore dark green pants, matching short-sleeved jacket, and an Akubra hat at rather a rakish angle.

Belligerent, Konrad demanded, "Who the hell are you?"

Norbert, who was frowning at me, ignored the

question. The shotgun he held on us remained steady. The light glanced off the delicate filigree engraving, and I realized it must be a collector's item.

Konrad said, "That shotgun you've got — it's Vince's."

Shifting his attention from my face to Konrad's, Norbert said, "Vince? Is that his name? He showed me the way down here."

Wade, ashen, spoke for the first time. "Then where is he?" His voice trembled.

"Over there, behind the rock."

There was silence for a moment, then Konrad said, "You've killed Vince?"

"Of course."

Wade made an inarticulate sound, then turned and bolted for the cliff. The crack of a shot split the air. The back of Wade's skull disintegrated. His churning legs failed him, and he pitched forward, smacking into the ground with sickening force. He twitched for a moment, then was still.

"I'm an excellent shot," said Norbert, "and I still have one shell to go before I reload." His tone was conversational, his expression pleasant. "I've come for my sister. Vince said she was arriving here by boat."

Konrad was disconcerted for a moment, then his face cleared. "Norbert Cummins."

"That's right. Where's Dana?"

Gesturing at me, Konrad said, "Here. Dana's dyed her hair and —"

"She's not my sister. Don't waste my time. Tell me where she is."

Konrad looked at me, then back to Norbert, then me again. "You're not Dana Wright?"

The water was only two strides away. I could swim like a fish, and if I could dive deep enough, the shotgun couldn't hurt me. I said urgently, "Konrad, he only has one cartridge to fire. He can't get us both."

Norbert chuckled. "But what if you're the one I get?" His expression hardened. "Sit down, both of you, close together."

Konrad lowered himself to the ground. I didn't, knowing that once I was down I'd have an even fainter chance of survival.

"Sit, or I'll blow your head off," Norbert said.

"If you do that," I noted reasonably, "you'll never know where Dana Wright is."

Norbert narrowed his blue eyes. "You know?"

"I know."

Konrad looked up at me, his face suffused with fury. "You fucking bitch. If you're not Dana, who are you?"

"Shut up," said Norbert. "You're boring me."

Konrad, literally grinding his teeth, continued to glare at me. "I'll rip you to pieces." His voice was a guttural growl.

I was surprised when Norbert stepped closer to us, because it gave Konrad and me a slightly better chance of tackling him. The gun was now trained on my body because I was still standing and therefore the principal threat.

Conversationally, Norbert said to Konrad. "Do you have any idea where my sister is? I must find her."

Konrad's rage swamped his caution. "No, you stupid bastard," he snarled. "I don't know where the fuck your sister is. I thought this bitch was her."

"So you won't be any help to me." A statement, not a question.

As Konrad opened his mouth to say something, Norbert discharged the second barrel directly into his face. Then, faster than I thought possible, he swung the still smoking gun at me.

The barrel struck me a glancing blow, but it was enough to make me stumble and fall. In a second he had broken the shotgun open and was reloading with fat cartridges he'd grabbed from the pocket of his jacket.

I crouched, gathered my strength, and launched myself at him, hitting him low in the gut with my left shoulder. We fell together at the water's edge, the shotgun clattering onto the rocks. I tried to seize it, but he was there first, and, wet and swearing, he got to his feet and leveled it at me. He'd lost his hat and some of his composure.

I stood up slowly. My heart was thudding so hard I felt it might shake me apart. I'd had a chance, and wasted it.

"I'll shatter your knee," Norbert said. "That should convince you to tell me exactly where Dana is."

I watched his finger tighten on the front trigger, and tensed to make one last attempt, when behind Norbert, like a gray nightmare rising from the water, a monstrous crocodile lunged at him.

The curve of its jaws giving it a ferocious open-mouthed smile, it caught Norbert at knee height. He shouted with surprise as he went down, both barrels of the shotgun discharging harmlessly into the air.

Twisting to see what had seized him, Norbert shrieked. He turned his face back to me, his eyes wide with horror. Stretched out his hand. "Help me! Help me!"

Involuntarily I reached for Norbert's extended

fingers, but with a massive heave of its squat, reptilian body, the crocodile hauld him into the water. He shrieked again, a dreadful, hopeless sound that battered against the hard stone walls.

Still with Norbert in its jaws, the creature rolled over, its paler belly uppermost for a brief moment.

Vince, who now lay dead a few meters from me, had lectured us on crocodiles. "And then it does a death roll," I heard his voice saying, "thrashing over to break your neck."

A rush of bubbles disturbed the surface, the last air from Norbert Cummins's lungs. Silence. I closed my eyes, unwilling to imagine what was happening out of sight in the cool, uncaring water.

CHAPTER TWENTY-FOUR

I checked that Vince was dead — insects were buzzing around the bloody stump that had once been his head — then clambered up to the top of the cliff. Everything seemed to me not quite authentic, as though I were in some immense virtual reality machine.

Corrina and Aaron met me on the last part of the track. "Dana, you're back!" Aaron exclaimed. "Have you seen Vince? Corrina and I just returned with supplies, and there seems to have been a struggle..."

Something in my face silenced him. Corrina said, "What's happened?"

"My brother's killed them all."

It was no surprise that even the violent deaths of four people did not induce Edification to advise the proper authorities. When Gary, Fergus, and Evonne arrived the next morning, the men went down to the gorge to remove and bury the bodies, Evonne having refused point-blank to have anything to do with the process.

They returned a couple of hours later with the news that Konrad's body had disappeared. "Crocs," said Gary tersely. This had given them the bright idea of disposing of the others by means of the food chain, so they'd hauled Wade and Vince to the water's edge and left them half floating there.

"Didn't see any salties," said Fergus, who apparently now regarded himself as sufficiently expert to refer to saltwater crocodiles in this familiar way, "but, Jesus, were we skittery when we got near the water!"

"Darl, don't look like that," said Gary, sympathetic. He glared at Fergus. "Dana saw her brother taken by a croc just yesterday, you stupid bastard."

I could hardly play the grieving sister, as everyone knew that Norbert had intended to kill me, but I could be badly shaken by the whole experience.

"I can't stay at the camp," I said. "Not after seeing . . ." I drooped a little. "It was more dreadful than you can imagine."

It wasn't an act. In reality I couldn't wait to get

away as far as possible from the place. Then maybe the scenes that played and replayed in my head would stop.

It took several weeks to follow all the leads that surveillance had provided, then in a coordinated action, national security agents struck in dawn raids to arrest members of Edification, including Larry in his Mosman mansion.

By this time Camp E had already disbanded, but everyone except Fergus and Mokhtar was tracked down. Fergus had returned to California, and somehow getting wind of what was happening, had disappeared over the border into Mexico before he could be picked up. Mokhtar was dead, having blown himself up while making a bomb in a Toronto apartment building.

The rest of my companions at Camp E — Patsy, Rob, Cliff, Evonne, Brit, Gary, and Joyce — were arrested. Joyce put up quite a fight, and had to be subdued with pepper spray. Brit, who'd been judged by the media as one of the most photogenic of the Edification arrestees, announced she had found God. As an added precaution she had also hired a formidable legal team to defend her.

After much behind-the-scenes angst in the national security ranks, the Hurdstone Peace Foundation was given public credit for assisting in the gutting of Edification. Siobhan was never identified as being associated with the Hurdstone Foundation, and to preserve her cover was taken into custody with all the others. She would only be used as a witness if absolutely necessary, but as a great deal of evidence had been amassed in the raids, this seemed unlikely.

Livia arranged for us to meet during Siobhan's ASIO debriefing. "And the room is clear," Livia assured me, with an annoyingly knowing expression on her face. "So you can talk freely."

Siobhan was standing by the window, and turned when I opened the door. Her looks were extraordinary, I decided. She never appeared exactly the same to me. It was as if the planes of her face could subtly change at will.

"Don't ask me to call you Mary," I said. "I've tried in my imagination, and it just doesn't work."

She smiled mockingly. "And you'll always be Dana to me."

"Now we've established that . . ." I bit my lip. "How long before you're free?"

She raised her shoulders. "Six months, maybe more. All the charges will ultimately be dropped for lack of evidence, but everything must seem legitimate. I can't continue my work if there's any suspicion I'm associated with the Foundation, or, pity help me, with your side of the fence."

"Would it sound crass to ask, What about us?"

She came close, slipped her arms about me. "Not crass, but rather hopeful."

We kissed, and the jolt went down to my toes. "Wow," I said, "you pack quite a punch."

She touched my cheek. "You've gone blond again, but I rather liked you with dark hair."

"Liar."

"Well . . ." Her smile faded. "I'm not lying about how I feel about you. But my father and the Hurdstone Foundation —"

"I understand."

We looked at each other for a long moment. She gave me a gorgeous smile. "Shall we meet undercover again some time?"

"It's a date," I said.

LOOKING FOR NAIAD?

Buy our books at
www.naiadpress.com

or call our toll-free number
1-800-533-1973

or by fax (24 hours a day)
1-850-539-9731

SHE WALKS IN BEAUTY by Nicole Conn. 304 pp. Meet
Spencer — she is talented, handsome, and driven to succeed.
ISBN 1-56280-269-0   **$14.95**

SUBSTITUTE FOR LOVE by Karin Kallmaker. 288 pp. Take one
look and fall hopelessly in lust.   ISBN 1-56280-265-8   12.95

OUT OF SIGHT by Claire McNab. 240 pp. 3rd Denise Cleever
thriller.   ISBN 1-56280-268-2   12.95

DEATH CLUB by Claire McNab. 224 pp. 13th Detective Inspector
Carol Ashton Mystery.   ISBN 1-56280-267-4   11.95

FROSTING ON THE CAKE by Karin Kallmaker. 272 pp.The
answer to every romance.   ISBN 1-56280-266-6   **$11.95**

DEATH UNDERSTOOD by Claire McNab. 240 pp. 2nd Denise
Cleever thriller.   ISBN 1-56280-264-X   **$11.95**

TREASURED PAST by Linda Hill. 208 pp. A shared passion for
antiques leads to love.   ISBN 1-56280-263-1   **$11.95**

UNDER SUSPICION by Claire McNab. 224 pp. 12th Detective
Inspector Carol Ashton mystery.   ISBN 1-56280-261-5   **$11.95**

UNFORGETTABLE by Karin Kallmaker. 288 pp. Can each
woman win her true love's heart?   ISBN 1-56280-260-7   12.95

MURDER UNDERCOVER by Claire McNab. 192 pp. 1st Denise
Cleever thriller.   ISBN 1-56280-259-3   12.95

EVERYTIME WE SAY GOODBYE by Jaye Maiman. 272 pp.
7th Robin Miller mystery.   ISBN 1-56280-248-8   11.95

SEVENTH HEAVEN by Kate Calloway. 240 pp. 7th Cassidy
James mystery.   ISBN 1-56280-262-3   11.95

STRANGERS IN THE NIGHT by Barbara Johnson. 208 pp. Her
body and soul react to a stranger's touch.   ISBN 1-56280-256-9   11.95

THE VERY THOUGHT OF YOU edited by Barbara Grier and
Christine Cassidy. 288 pp. Erotic love stories by Naiad Press
authors.   ISBN 1-56280-250-X   14.95

TO HAVE AND TO HOLD by Peggy J. Herring. 192 pp. Their
friendship grows to intense passion . . .   ISBN 1-56280-251-8   11.95

INTIMATE STRANGER by Laura DeHart Young. 192 pp.
Ignoring Tray's myserious past, could Cole be playing with fire?
                                      ISBN 1-56280-249-6   11.95

SHATTERED ILLUSIONS by Kaye Davis. 256 pp. 4th
Maris Middleton mystery.   ISBN 1-56280-252-6   11.95

SET UP by Claire McNab. 224 pp. 11th Detective Inspector Carol
Ashton mystery.   ISBN 1-56280-255-0   11.95

THE DAWNING by Laura Adams. 224 pp. What if you had the
power to change the past?   ISBN 1-56280-246-1   11.95

NEVER ENDING by Marianne K. Martin. 224 pp. Temptation
appears in the form of an old friend and lover. ISBN 1-56280-247-X   11.95

ONE OF OUR OWN by Diane Salvatore. 240 pp. Carly Matson
has a secret. So does Lela Johns.   ISBN 1-56280-243-7   11.95

DOUBLE TAKEOUT by Tracey Richardson. 176 pp. 3rd Stevie
Houston mystery.   ISBN 1-56280-244-5   11.95

CAPTIVE HEART by Frankie J. Jones. 176 pp. Love in the
fast lane or heartside romance?   ISBN 1-56280-258-5   11.95

WICKED GOOD TIME by Diana Tremain Braund. 224 pp. In
charge at work, out of control in her heart. ISBN 1-56280-241-0   11.95

SNAKE EYES by Pat Welch. 256 pp. 7th Helen Black mystery.
                                      ISBN 1-56280-242-9   11.95

CHANGE OF HEART by Linda Hill. 176 pp. High fashion and
love in a glamorous world.   ISBN 1-56280-238-0   11.95

UNSTRUNG HEART by Robbi Sommers. 176 pp. Putting life
in order again.   ISBN 1-56280-239-9   11.95

BIRDS OF A FEATHER by Jackie Calhoun. 240 pp. Life begins
with love.   ISBN 1-56280-240-2   11.95

THE DRIVE by Trisha Todd. 176 pp. The star of *Claire of the
Moon* tells all!   ISBN 1-56280-237-2   11.95

BOTH SIDES by Saxon Bennett. 240 pp. A community of
women falling in and out of love.   ISBN 1-56280-236-4   11.95

WATERMARK by Karin Kallmaker. 256 pp. One burning
question . . . how to lead her back to love? ISBN 1-56280-235-6   11.95

SILVER THREADS by Lyn Denison.208 pp. Finding her way
back to love . . .   ISBN 1-56280-231-3   11.95

CHIMNEY ROCK BLUES by Janet McClellan. 224 pp. 4th Tru
North mystery.   ISBN 1-56280-233-X   11.95

OMAHA'S BELL by Penny Hayes. 208 pp. Orphaned Keeley
Delaney woos the lovely Prudence Morris.　　ISBN 1-56280-232-1　　11.95

SIXTH SENSE by Kate Calloway. 224 pp. 6th Cassidy James
mystery.　　ISBN 1-56280-228-3　　11.95

DAWN OF THE DANCE by Marianne K. Martin. 224 pp. A dance
with an old friend, nothing more . . . yeah!　　ISBN 1-56280-229-1　　11.95

THOSE WHO WAIT by Peggy J. Herring. 160 pp. Two
sisters . . . in love with the same woman.　　ISBN 1-56280-223-2　　11.95

WHISPERS IN THE WIND by Frankie J. Jones. 192 pp. "If you
don't want this," she whispered, "all you have to say is 'stop.' "
　　ISBN 1-56280-226-7　　11.95

WHEN SOME BODY DISAPPEARS by Therese Szymanski.
192 pp. 3rd Brett Higgins mystery.　　ISBN 1-56280-227-5　　11.95

UNTIL THE END by Kaye Davis. 256pp. 3rd Maris Middleton
mystery.　　ISBN 1-56280-222-4　　11.95

FIFTH WHEEL by Kate Calloway. 224 pp. 5th Cassidy James
mystery.　　ISBN 1-56280-218-6　　11.95

JUST YESTERDAY by Linda Hill. 176 pp. Reliving all the
passion of yesterday.　　ISBN 1-56280-219-4　　11.95

THE TOUCH OF YOUR HAND edited by Barbara Grier and
Christine Cassidy. 304 pp. Erotic love stories by Naiad Press
authors.　　ISBN 1-56280-220-8　　14.95

PAST DUE by Claire McNab. 224 pp. 10th Carol Ashton
mystery.　　ISBN 1-56280-217-8　　11.95

CHRISTABEL by Laura Adams. 224 pp. Two captive hearts and
the passion that will set them free.　　ISBN 1-56280-214-3　　11.95

PRIVATE PASSIONS by Laura DeHart Young. 192 pp. An
unforgettable new portrait of lesbian love . . .　　ISBN 1-56280-215-1　　11.95

BAD MOON RISING by Barbara Johnson. 208 pp. 2nd Colleen
Fitzgerald mystery.　　ISBN 1-56280-211-9　　11.95

RIVER QUAY by Janet McClellan. 208 pp. 3rd Tru North
mystery.　　ISBN 1-56280-212-7　　11.95

ENDLESS LOVE by Lisa Shapiro. 272 pp. To believe, once
again, that love can be forever.　　ISBN 1-56280-213-5　　11.95

FALLEN FROM GRACE by Pat Welch. 256 pp. 6th Helen Black
mystery.　　ISBN 1-56280-209-7　　11.95

OVER THE LINE by Tracey Richardson. 176 pp. 2nd Stevie
Houston mystery.　　ISBN 1-56280-202-X　　11.95

LOVE IN THE BALANCE by Marianne K. Martin. 256 pp.
Weighing the costs of love . . .　　ISBN 1-56280-199-6　　11.95

PIECE OF MY HEART by Julia Watts. 208 pp. All the
stuff that dreams are made of —　　ISBN 1-56280-206-2　　11.95

MAKING UP FOR LOST TIME by Karin Kallmaker. 240 pp.
Nobody does it better . . .   ISBN 1-56280-196-1   11.95

GOLD FEVER by Lyn Denison. 224 pp. By author of *Dream
Lover*.   ISBN 1-56280-201-1   11.95

WHEN THE DEAD SPEAK by Therese Szymanski. 224 pp. 2nd
Brett Higgins mystery.   ISBN 1-56280-198-8   11.95

FOURTH DOWN by Kate Calloway. 240 pp. 4th Cassidy James
mystery.   ISBN 1-56280-193-7   11.95

CITY LIGHTS COUNTRY CANDLES by Penny Hayes. 208 pp.
About the women she has known . . .   ISBN 1-56280-195-3   11.95

POSSESSIONS by Kaye Davis. 240 pp. 2nd Maris Middleton
mystery.   ISBN 1-56280-192-9   11.95

A QUESTION OF LOVE by Saxon Bennett. 208 pp. Every
woman is granted one great love.   ISBN 1-56280-205-4   11.95

RHYTHM TIDE by Frankie J. Jones. 160 pp.   . . . to desire
passionately and be passionately desired.   ISBN 1-56280-189-9   11.95

PENN VALLEY PHOENIX by Janet McClellan. 208 pp. 2nd
Tru North Mystery.   ISBN 1-56280-200-3   11.95

OLD BLACK MAGIC by Jaye Maiman. 272 pp. 6th Robin
Miller mystery.   ISBN 1-56280-175-9   11.95

LADY BE GOOD edited by Barbara Grier and Christine Cassidy.
288 pp. Erotic stories by Naiad Press authors. ISBN 1-56280-180-5   14.95

CHAIN LETTER by Claire McNab. 288 pp. 9th Carol Ashton
mystery.   ISBN 1-56280-181-3   11.95

NIGHT VISION by Laura Adams. 256 pp. Erotic fantasy romance
by "famous" author.   ISBN 1-56280-182-1   11.95

SEA TO SHINING SEA by Lisa Shapiro. 256 pp. Unable to resist
the raging passion . . .   ISBN 1-56280-177-5   11.95

THIRD DEGREE by Kate Calloway. 224 pp. 3rd Cassidy James
mystery.   ISBN 1-56280-185-6   11.95

WHEN THE DANCING STOPS by Therese Szymanski. 272 pp.
1st Brett Higgins mystery.   ISBN 1-56280-186-4   11.95

PHASES OF THE MOON by Julia Watts. 192 pp. . . . . hungry
for everything life has to offer.   ISBN 1-56280-176-7   11.95

BABY IT'S COLD by Jaye Maiman. 256 pp. 5th Robin Miller
mystery.   ISBN 1-56280-156-2   10.95

CLASS REUNION by Linda Hill. 176 pp. The girl from her
past . . .   ISBN 1-56280-178-3   11.95

FORTY LOVE by Diana Simmonds. 288 pp. Joyous, heart-
warming romance.   ISBN 1-56280-171-6   11.95

IN THE MOOD by Robbi Sommers. 160 pp. The queen of
erotic tension!   ISBN 1-56280-172-4   11.95

SWIMMING CAT COVE by Lauren Wright Douglas. 192 pp. 2nd
Allison O'Neil Mystery.   ISBN 1-56280-168-6   11.95

THE LOVING LESBIAN by Claire McNab and Sharon Gedan.
240 pp. Explore the experiences that make lesbian love unique.
                                                  ISBN 1-56280-169-4   14.95

SEASONS OF THE HEART by Jackie Calhoun. 240 pp. Romance
through the years.   ISBN 1-56280-167-8   11.95

K. C. BOMBER by Janet McClellan. 208 pp. 1st Tru North
mystery.   ISBN 1-56280-157-0   11.95

LAST RITES by Tracey Richardson. 192 pp. 1st Stevie Houston
mystery.   ISBN 1-56280-164-3   11.95

EMBRACE IN MOTION by Karin Kallmaker. 256 pp. A whirlwind
love affair.   ISBN 1-56280-165-1   11.95

HOT CHECK by Peggy J. Herring. 192 pp. Will workaholic Alice
fall for guitarist Ricky?   ISBN 1-56280-163-5   11.95

OLD TIES by Saxon Bennett. 176 pp. Can Cleo surrender to a
passionate new love?   ISBN 1-56280-159-7   11.95

SECOND FIDDLE by Kate Kalloway. 208 pp. 2nd P.I. Cassidy James
mystery.   ISBN 1-56280-161-9   11.95

LAUREL by Isabel Miller. 128 pp. By the author of the beloved
Patience and Sarah.   ISBN 1-56280-146-5   10.95

LOVE OR MONEY by Jackie Calhoun. 240 pp. The romance of
real life.   ISBN 1-56280-147-3   10.95

SMOKE AND MIRRORS by Pat Welch. 224 pp. 5th Helen Black
Mystery.   ISBN 1-56280-143-0   10.95

DANCING IN THE DARK edited by Barbara Grier & Christine
Cassidy. 272 pp. Erotic love stories by Naiad Press authors.
                                                  ISBN 1-56280-144-9   14.95

TIME AND TIME AGAIN by Catherine Ennis. 176 pp. Passionate
love affair.   ISBN 1-56280-145-7   10.95

PAXTON COURT by Diane Salvatore. 256 pp. Erotic and wickedly
funny contemporary tale about the business of learning to live
together.   ISBN 1-56280-114-7   10.95

INNER CIRCLE by Claire McNab. 208 pp. 8th Carol Ashton
Mystery.   ISBN 1-56280-135-X   11.95

LESBIAN SEX: AN ORAL HISTORY by Susan Johnson.
240 pp. Need we say more?   ISBN 1-56280-142-2   14.95

WILD THINGS by Karin Kallmaker. 240 pp. By the undisputed
mistress of lesbian romance.   ISBN 1-56280-139-2   12.95

NOW AND THEN by Penny Hayes. 240 pp. Romance on the
westward journey.   ISBN 1-56280-121-X   11.95

DEATH AT LAVENDER BAY by Lauren Wright Douglas. 208 pp. 1st Allison O'Neil Mystery.   ISBN 1-56280-085-X   11.95

YES I SAID YES I WILL by Judith McDaniel. 272 pp. Hot romance by famous author.   ISBN 1-56280-138-4   11.95

FORBIDDEN FIRES by Margaret C. Anderson. Edited by Mathilda Hills. 176 pp. Famous author's "unpublished" Lesbian romance.
ISBN 1-56280-123-6   21.95

WILDWOOD FLOWERS by Julia Watts. 208 pp. Hilarious and heart-warming tale of true love.   ISBN 1-56280-127-9   10.95

NEVER SAY NEVER by Linda Hill. 224 pp. Rule #1: Never get involved with . . .   ISBN 1-56280-126-0   11.95

THE WISH LIST by Saxon Bennett. 192 pp. Romance through the years.   ISBN 1-56280-125-2   10.95

FAMILY SECRETS by Laura DeHart Young. 208 pp. Enthralling romance and suspense.   ISBN 1-56280-119-8   10.95

INLAND PASSAGE by Jane Rule. 288 pp. Tales exploring conventional & unconventional relationships.   ISBN 0-930044-56-8   10.95

DOUBLE BLUFF by Claire McNab. 208 pp. 7th Carol Ashton Mystery.   ISBN 1-56280-096-5   12.95

THE FIRST TIME EVER edited by Barbara Grier & Christine Cassidy. 272 pp. Love stories by Naiad Press authors.
ISBN 1-56280-086-8   14.95

CHANGES by Jackie Calhoun. 208 pp. Involved romance and relationships.   ISBN 1-56280-083-3   10.95

GETTING THERE by Robbi Sommers. 192 pp. Nobody does it like Robbi!   ISBN 1-56280-099-X   10.95

FLASHPOINT by Katherine V. Forrest. 256 pp. A Lesbian blockbuster!   ISBN 1-56280-079-5   10.95

CLAIRE OF THE MOON by Nicole Conn. Audio Book — Read by Marianne Hyatt.   ISBN 1-56280-113-9   13.95

FOR LOVE AND FOR LIFE: INTIMATE PORTRAITS OF LESBIAN COUPLES by Susan Johnson. 224 pp.
ISBN 1-56280-091-4   14.95

SOMEONE TO WATCH by Jaye Maiman. 272 pp. 4th Robin Miller Mystery.   ISBN 1-56280-095-7   10.95

TRAVELS WITH DIANA HUNTER by Regine Sands. Erotic lesbian romp. Audio Book (2 cassettes)   ISBN 1-56280-107-4   13.95

CABIN FEVER by Carol Schmidt. 256 pp. Sizzling suspense and passion.   ISBN 1-56280-089-1   10.95

THERE WILL BE NO GOODBYES by Laura DeHart Young. 192 pp. Romantic love, strength, and friendship.   ISBN 1-56280-103-1   10.95

FAULTLINE by Sheila Ortiz Taylor. 144 pp. Joyous comic
lesbian novel.   ISBN 1-56280-108-2   9.95

OPEN HOUSE by Pat Welch. 176 pp. 4th Helen Black Mystery.
                                         ISBN 1-56280-102-3   10.95

PAINTED MOON by Karin Kallmaker. 224 pp. Delicious
Kallmaker romance.   ISBN 1-56280-075-2   12.95

THE MYSTERIOUS NAIAD edited by Katherine V. Forrest &
Barbara Grier. 320 pp. Love stories by Naiad Press authors.
                                         ISBN 1-56280-074-4   14.95

DAUGHTERS OF A CORAL DAWN by Katherine V. Forrest.
240 pp. Tenth Anniversay Edition.   ISBN 1-56280-104-X   11.95

BODY GUARD by Claire McNab. 208 pp. 6th Carol Ashton
Mystery.   ISBN 1-56280-073-6   11.95

SECOND GUESS by Rose Beecham. 216 pp. An Amanda
Valentine Mystery.   ISBN 1-56280-069-8   9.95

A RAGE OF MAIDENS by Lauren Wright Douglas. 240 pp.
6th Caitlin Reece Mystery.   ISBN 1-56280-068-X   10.95

TRIPLE EXPOSURE by Jackie Calhoun. 224 pp. Romantic
drama involving many characters.   ISBN 1-56280-067-1   10.95

PERSONAL ADS by Robbi Sommers. 176 pp. Sizzling short
stories.   ISBN 1-56280-059-0   11.95

SWEET CHERRY WINE by Carol Schmidt. 224 pp. A novel of
suspense.   ISBN 1-56280-063-9   9.95

KATHLEEN O'DONALD by Penny Hayes. 256 pp. Rose and
Kathleen find each other and employment in 1909 NYC.
                                         ISBN 1-56280-070-1   9.95

STAYING HOME by Elisabeth Nonas. 256 pp. Molly and Alix
want a baby . . . or do they?   ISBN 1-56280-076-0   10.95

TRUE LOVE by Jennifer Fulton. 240 pp. Six lesbians searching
for love in all the "right" places.   ISBN 1-56280-035-3   11.95

THE ROMANTIC NAIAD edited by Katherine V. Forrest &
Barbara Grier. 336 pp. Love stories by Naiad Press authors.
                                         ISBN 1-56280-054-X   14.95

UNDER MY SKIN by Jaye Maiman. 336 pp. 3rd Robin Miller
Mystery.   ISBN 1-56280-049-3.   11.95

CAR POOL by Karin Kallmaker. 272pp. Lesbians on wheels
and then some!   ISBN 1-56280-048-5   11.95

NOT TELLING MOTHER: STORIES FROM A LIFE by Diane
Salvatore. 176 pp. Her 3rd novel.   ISBN 1-56280-044-2   9.95

GOBLIN MARKET by Lauren Wright Douglas. 240pp. 5th Caitlin
Reece Mystery.   ISBN 1-56280-047-7   10.95

BEHIND CLOSED DOORS by Robbi Sommers. 192 pp. Hot,
erotic short stories. ISBN 1-56280-039-6 11.95

CLAIRE OF THE MOON by Nicole Conn. 192 pp. See the
movie — read the book! ISBN 1-56280-038-8 11.95

SILENT HEART by Claire McNab. 192 pp. Exotic Lesbian
romance. ISBN 1-56280-036-1 11.95

SAVING GRACE by Jennifer Fulton. 240 pp. Adventure and
romantic entanglement. ISBN 1-56280-051-5 11.95

CURIOUS WINE by Katherine V. Forrest. 176 pp. Tenth Anniver-
sary Edition. The most popular contemporary Lesbian love story.
ISBN 1-56280-053-1 11.95
   Audio Book (2 cassettes) ISBN 1-56280-105-8 13.95

A PROPER BURIAL by Pat Welch. 192 pp. 3rd Helen Black
Mystery. ISBN 1-56280-033-7 9.95

LOVE, ZENA BETH by Diane Salvatore. 224 pp. The most talked
about lesbian novel of the nineties! ISBN 1-56280-030-2 10.95

A DOORYARD FULL OF FLOWERS by Isabel Miller. 160 pp.
Stories incl. 2 sequels to *Patience and Sarah.* ISBN 1-56280-029-9 9.95

MURDER BY TRADITION by Katherine V. Forrest. 288 pp. 4th
Kate Delafield Mystery. ISBN 1-56280-002-7 11.95

THE EROTIC NAIAD edited by Katherine V. Forrest & Barbara
Grier. 224 pp. Love stories by Naiad Press authors.
ISBN 1-56280-026-4 14.95

DEAD CERTAIN by Claire McNab. 224 pp. 5th Carol Ashton
Mystery. ISBN 1-56280-027-2 11.95

CRAZY FOR LOVING by Jaye Maiman. 320 pp. 2nd Robin Miller
Mystery. ISBN 1-56280-025-6 11.95

UNCERTAIN COMPANIONS by Robbi Sommers. 204 pp.
Steamy, erotic novel. ISBN 1-56280-017-5 11.95

A TIGER'S HEART by Lauren Wright Douglas. 240 pp. 4th Caitlin
Reece Mystery. ISBN 1-56280-018-3 9.95

PAPERBACK ROMANCE by Karin Kallmaker. 256 pp. A
delicious romance. ISBN 1-56280-019-1 11.95

THE LAVENDER HOUSE MURDER by Nikki Baker. 224 pp.
2nd Virginia Kelly Mystery. ISBN 1-56280-012-4 9.95

PASSION BAY by Jennifer Fulton. 224 pp. Passionate romance,
virgin beaches, tropical skies. ISBN 1-56280-028-0 11.95

STICKS AND STONES by Jackie Calhoun. Contemporary
lesbian lives and loves.
Audio Book (2 cassettes) ISBN 1-56280-106-6 13.95

UNDER THE SOUTHERN CROSS by Claire McNab. 192 pp.
Romantic nights Down Under. ISBN 1-56280-011-6 11.95

PLEASURES by Robbi Sommers. 204 pp. Unprecedented
eroticism. ISBN 0-941483-49-5 11.95

FATAL REUNION by Claire McNab. 224 pp. 2nd Carol Ashton
Mystery. ISBN 0-941483-40-1 11.95

IN EVERY PORT by Karin Kallmaker. 228 pp. Jessica's sexy,
adventuresome travels. ISBN 0-941483-34-7 12.95

OF LOVE AND GLORY by Evelyn Kennedy. 192 pp. Exciting
WWII romance. ISBN 0-941483-32-0 10.95

CLICKING STONES by Nancy Tyler Glenn. 288 pp. Love
transcending time. ISBN 0-941483-31-2 9.95

SOUTH OF THE LINE by Catherine Ennis. 216 pp. Civil War
adventure. ISBN 0-941483-29-0 8.95

THE FINER GRAIN by Denise Ohio. 216 pp. Brilliant young
college lesbian novel. ISBN 0-941483-11-8 8.95

LESSONS IN MURDER by Claire McNab. 216 pp. 1st Carol Ashton
Mystery. ISBN 0-941483-14-2 11.95

YELLOWTHROAT by Penny Hayes. 240 pp. Margarita, bandit,
kidnaps Julia. ISBN 0-941483-10-X 8.95

SAPPHISTRY: THE BOOK OF LESBIAN SEXUALITY by
Pat Califia. 3d edition, revised. 208 pp. ISBN 0-941483-24-X 12.95

TO THE LIGHTNING by Catherine Ennis. 208 pp. Romantic
Lesbian `Robinson Crusoe adventure. ISBN 0-941483-06-1 8.95

DREAMS AND SWORDS by Katherine V. Forrest. 192 pp.
Romantic, erotic, imaginative stories. ISBN 0-941483-03-7 11.95

MEMORY BOARD by Jane Rule. 336 pp. Memorable novel
about an aging Lesbian couple. ISBN 0-941483-02-9 12.95

THE LONG TRAIL by Penny Hayes. 248 pp. Vivid adventures
of two women in love in the old west. ISBN 0-930044-76-2 8.95

DESERT OF THE HEART by Jane Rule. 224 pp. A classic;
basis for the movie *Desert Hearts*. ISBN 0-930044-73-8 12.95

SEX VARIANT WOMEN IN LITERATURE by Jeannette
Howard Foster. 448 pp. Literary history. ISBN 0-930044-65-7 8.95

A HOT-EYED MODERATE by Jane Rule. 252 pp. Hard-hitting
essays on gay life; writing; art. ISBN 0-930044-57-6 7.95

AMATEUR CITY by Katherine V. Forrest. 224 pp. 1st Kate
Delafield Mystery. ISBN 0-930044-55-X 11.95

THE YOUNG IN ONE ANOTHER'S ARMS by Jane Rule.
224 pp. Classic Jane Rule. ISBN 0-930044-53-3 9.95

AGAINST THE SEASON by Jane Rule. 224 pp. Luminous,
complex novel of interrelationships. ISBN 0-930044-48-7 8.95

THIS IS NOT FOR YOU by Jane Rule. 284 pp. A letter to a
beloved is also an intricate novel. ISBN 0-930044-25-8 8.95

OUTLANDER by Jane Rule. 207 pp. Short stories and essays by
one of our finest writers.   ISBN 0-930044-17-7   8.95

These are just a few of the many Naiad Press titles — we are the oldest and
largest lesbian/feminist publishing company in the world. We also offer an
enormous selection of lesbian video products. Please request a complete
catalog. We offer personal service; we encourage and welcome direct mail
orders from individuals who have limited access to bookstores carrying our
publications.